CW00919292

Whose dark or troubled mind will you step into next? Detective or assassin, victim or accomplice? How can you tell reality from delusion when you're spinning in the whirl of a thriller, or trapped in the grip of an unsolvable mystery? When you can't trust your senses, or anyone you meet; that's when you know you're in the hands of the undisputed masters of crime fiction.

Writers of the greatest thrillers and mysteries on earth, who inspired those that followed. Their books are found on shelves all across their home countries—from Asia to Europe, and everywhere in between. Timeless tales that have been devoured, adored and handed down through the decades. Iconic books that have inspired films, and demand to be read and read again. And now we've introduced Pushkin Vertigo Originals—the greatest contemporary crime writing from across the globe, by some of today's best authors.

So step inside a dizzying world of criminal masterminds with **Pushkin Vertigo**. The only trouble you might have is leaving them behind.

PUSHKIN VERTIGO

DEATH GOING

DOWN

TRANSLATED BY LUCY GREAVES

MARÍA
ANGÉLICA BOSCO

Work published within the framework of "Sur" Translation Support Program
of the Ministry of Foreign Affairs and Worship of the Argentine Republic.

Obra editada en el marco del Programa "Sur" de Apoyo a las Traducciones del Ministerio
de Relaciones Exteriores y Culto de la República Argentina.

Pushkin Vertigo
71–75 Shelton Street
London, WC2H 9JQ

Original text © Julian Gil, 1955

First published in Spanish as *La muerte baja en ascensor*
by Emecé Editores in 1955

Translation © Lucy Greaves, 2016
First published by Pushkin Vertigo in 2016

1 3 5 7 9 8 6 4 2

ISBN 978 1 782272 23 6

All rights reserved. No part of this publication may be reproduced,
stored in a retrieval system or transmitted in any form or by
any means electronic, mechanical, photocopying, recording or
otherwise, without prior permission in writing from Pushkin Press

Text designed and typeset by Tetragon, London
Printed and bound by CPI Group (UK) Ltd, Croydon CR0 4YY

www.pushkinpress.com

CONTENTS

1

Death Going Down

The car pulled up in front of an apartment building on one of the first blocks of Calle Santa Fe, where the street opens out to a view across the wide Plaza San Martín. At two in the morning on that cold, misty August night, only the occasional vehicle was gliding over the damp shiny asphalt.

The few people walking the streets were silhouetted against a desolate background. They hurried along, harassed by the temperature and the late hour, but moved with the uncertain gait of sleepwalkers. They were spurred on by the desire to get home, wherever that was, because when night and winter reign in the streets and there is a sense of others sleeping behind closed windows, whether peacefully or fitfully, even a room that is lonely or filled with painful memories counts as home.

Pancho Soler let his body fall against the car door to open it. Framed by the windscreen, the double row of buildings seemed to go on without end. A wave of nausea forced him to close his eyes and steady himself. When he opened them again a yellow streetlamp swam into focus, looking like a badly painted moon.

A pair of legs, floppy as if made of cloth, emerged from the car door and Soler thrust his face into the frozen night air like a carp bursting out of water. The pavement stretched from the car to the building door like an abyss of dull slabs, filling him with fear. He resolved to cross the space, trying in vain to give some direction to his disconnected footsteps, furious that the simplest of tasks demanded such concentration.

Still, he'd had a good time. He always had a good time with Luisita. She was a great girl who knew how to appreciate a drink, a useful tool to curb her eventual complaints. Women always complain that they are left alone.

The light in the lobby was on. If he hurried he would reach the lift before the regulation three minutes were up. The illuminated panel showed number six, the caretaker's apartment. What a nuisance! He would end up in the dark before the lift reached the ground floor.

Leaning on the frosted glass door, Soler waited while the red buttons lit up and went out successively. A fuzzy tiredness crept along his limbs and up into his head. All of a sudden he noticed that the lift shaft had filled with light and at the same moment, as if choreographed, the lobby plunged into darkness.

Someone had come down in the lift. He could make out a blurry shape on the other side of the door. Still leaning on the wall, Pancho moved to one side to make way for the person in the lift but the door remained stubbornly closed. All he could see was the shadow puppet outline of a shape curled up in the corner.

"It must be a woman," grumbled Soler. "Women always expect a chap to do everything."

Nonetheless, he pulled the door open with a smile in reserve in case it was indeed a woman. She might be young and pretty. The mirror doubled the unseemly position of the stranger, who was bundled up in a dark fur coat. He had already been softened

8

by alcohol, and the female shape, half collapsed against the back panel, somehow moved him. She showed not the slightest intention of moving from that spot. Poor thing, she must have been feeling even worse than he did.

There was an air of unreality as Soler, in his impulse for solidarity, approached the woman and saw she was young and blonde. She looked awfully pale. His annoyance faded as he noticed successive details. His selfishness was not, after all, the product of an adult's resentful attitude, but rather of a child's innocent self-interest.

All that bothered him now was the constant shifting of the walls and the ghostly light reflected by the mirror illuminating the fallen woman, with her face half hidden in the collar of her fur coat. A strand of blond hair hung limply across her cheek in a suggestion of intimacy. Soler stretched out his hand to sweep her hair back and in doing so, his fingers brushed against her skin. A spasm of horror froze him. Unaware of what he was doing, Soler reached out to touch the stranger's hands. He was surprised by his involuntary invocation:

"My God!"

He became aware of the ground becoming firmer under his feet. His face in the mirror looked strange and distorted, and the unlit lobby was like a shadowy pit where one wakes at the edge of nightmare. He felt a desperate need to shout in protest. Why did this have to happen to him, him of all people? If only Luisita had insisted he stay with her! That would have been less trouble, all things considered.

He then felt his legs bump against a smooth edge. He had stepped back as if the surprise had pushed him in the chest, and was now crashing against the chestnut-coloured velvet divan along the length of the lobby wall. Soler let himself fall onto it, his eyes fixed on the scene in the lift, which with distance was now brought into clearer focus.

Adolfo Luchter crossed Calle Santa Fe almost at a run, the cold biting his cheeks, bearing the unwelcome memory of desolate nights, and the next day looming as an arduous string of bitter hours to fight through in that unfamiliar city.

As he was about to open the front door he noticed Soler draped pitifully over the divan in the lobby. It was always the same! Whenever he arrived home late at night he ran into one of that man's displays of extravagant boredom. Soler would either be at home making merry with others just as convinced as he that to sleep at certain times of night denotes an utter lack of personality, or else one had to collect him at the door, help him up to his apartment and even put him into bed when the aforementioned displays had been excessive. Luchter was generally a helpful soul but his goodwill faltered when it came to people like Soler who took life for nothing more than a bothersome, illicit game.

Soler launched himself at the doctor when he saw him come in. Luchter was forced to grab him to prevent his fall, and noticed his glassy eyes. A slight shift of his blond eyebrows was the only sign of annoyance.

Luchter went to turn on the light. Soler clung to his arm, almost letting himself be dragged along. He muttered a few garbled words as though his tongue had to contort itself in his mouth in order to articulate them. His outstretched hand motioned towards the lift. From the gesture, more than from his speech, Luchter guessed what he was trying to say:

"Look," he mumbled, "there… there's a dead woman…"

The light came on and its brightness swept away the absurdity of those words, making them seem ridiculous.

"Stop all this silli—" Luchter started.

But a brief glance at the lift made him pause. He held back an exclamation of surprise and started towards the motionless woman. Soler stumbled behind him, following his steps and trying in vain to imitate his confident movements. Luchter would have liked to shoo him away but another more serious problem demanded his attention. Dr Luchter promptly bent forward to examine the stranger in the lift. He acted with an impersonal and professional efficiency. When he stood up, his clear green gaze was clouded with unease. He turned to see Soler's face, full of idiotic expectation.

"Was she with you?" he asked.

"No, no… I found her there… I've no idea who she is."

Again the light went off and the square of the lift stood out once more. Luchter's voice was clipped with anxiety.

"Did you see which floor the lift was stopped at when you called it?"

"The sixth… yes, the sixth."

"The caretaker's apartment. It makes no sense," the doctor muttered. Staring at the pathetic figure, he noticed the handbag beside her. He bent to pick it up.

"Don't touch it," whimpered Soler.

"Why not?"

"The police… what'll they say? We have to report it."

Fear, a wretched fear, weakened Soler's voice. That was the end of his game of cops and robbers. Now the thought of police uniforms seemed dreadful. Luchter shrugged.

"We've nothing to lose by trying to find out who she is. She might have lived in this building."

"Lived?"

Luchter, who had opened the handbag, let the anxious suspense of that question hang in the air. Soler then moved towards him. Well, if they must do something. He tried to peek over the doctor's shoulder.

"Leave me be," Luchter pushed him away harshly, making Soler lose his balance. To stop himself from falling, Soler snatched at the doctor's sleeve. Luchter stumbled and there was a metallic tinkling, like a muffled, mocking laugh. The bag's contents had spilt across the floor.

Wide-eyed, Soler contemplated the sudden appearance of those tiny objects: a powder compact, a handkerchief, a change purse, a wallet, an address book. Something rolled towards the gap beneath the door—a little golden tube, clearly a lipstick. It was going to disappear! Dear God, that was the same as admitting to having opened the bag! They heard no accusatory click as it fell, but it had disappeared all the same, silently and definitively.

"Did you see?" groaned Soler. "What now?"

Luchter was much calmer.

"It doesn't matter. They'll get it out later. Come with me, Soler."

Soler muttered a protest against going anywhere.

"So… she's dead, then? She's really dead?"

He pointed to the woman with an incredulous gesture. A person didn't just die like that, in a lift, at that time of night. How long would the formalities take? He needed to sleep. He heard Luchter answering the question he'd almost forgotten he'd asked.

"Yes, she's dead."

"How?"

"It looks like poisoning. There's a smell of bitter almonds. It must have been potassium cyanide."

Luchter took Soler's arm.

"We'll go up in the service lift," he said, dragging Soler along. "We have to tell the caretaker and the police. Come on."

The bell rang in the caretaker's apartment. Andrés Torres, half asleep, stretched out his hand towards the light as if the intermittent, high-pitched sound tugged at his arm. With the glare, his wife's dishevelled head emerged from under the blankets. Aurora had the same interrogatory appearance as the light that now filled the room.

Torres's next action put him in possession of his trousers, which had been waiting at the foot of the bed for him get up. He hurriedly pulled them on in order to recover the sense of individuality lost in sleep, obeying that simple, pathetic relationship between the clock and consciousness. He heard but did not understand what Dr Luchter was explaining through the door. Something about a body in the lift and the police, none of which fitted with his job as caretaker, who at six in the morning must set methodically to work and begin the daily battle with suppliers and residents. He turned to his wife and shot her an authoritative look with which he hoped to resolve his inner confusion.

"My goodness!" cried Aurora, jumping out of bed and grabbing her clothes, her face puffy from interrupted sleep,

"What are you doing, woman?" asked her husband.

"Getting dressed. I'm going down with you."

"No one called for you."

"I'm not staying here alone, not even on Saint James's orders. Didn't they say someone's been killed? The murderer's probably on the loose."

Torres paused with his hand still in the air, pulling at the elastic of his braces while trying to button them.

"Rubbish! Who said anything about a crime?"

"Well, I mean, if there's a body..."

Torres scratched his head. Feeling defeated, he turned to prophecy.

"That's what happens to people who go out at night. Just look how they end up. That's what my mother always said."

This was his worst complaint against his wife. Once a week, Aurora asked him to take her to an evening cinema screening. Pleased that the circumstances finally backed him up, he added:

"No good comes from roaming the streets at the sort of time when decent people are at home."

Aurora listened with her head bowed. The main thing was for her husband not to leave her alone. She even felt able to accept him turning her mother-in-law into a prophet of doom.

"Come on, Andrés, take me with you. I'm scared half to death."

She was lying. Something stronger than fear had taken hold of her. She mentally ran through the faces of the people who lived in the building, pausing with morbid pleasure on the ones she most disliked. Who could the victim be?

The police had arrived by the time they got down to the lobby. Two officers were guarding the main door. A corpulent middle-aged man and another younger man were taking a statement from Soler. Luchter was standing to one side, waiting his turn.

"Officer Vera," said the older man to the other, "notify Public Assistance to come for the body once the police surgeon has examined it. Call Inspector Ericourt, too. I'll carry on taking statements."

The officer saluted.

"You can use my telephone, Superintendent," offered Luchter.

"Thank you. Is someone there to open the door?"

"The cook."

"Go ahead, Officer Vera. Fifth floor, isn't it? And you, I need you now. What's your name?"

"Adolfo Luchter. Doctor."

"Argentinian?"

"Naturalized Argentinian. I've lived in this country for nine years."

"Please tell me what happened."

"I was coming home after leaving my car in the garage."

"Do you recall the time?"

"Approximately two fifteen. At two a.m. I left the house of a colleague with whom I was working on a report for the Neuropsychiatric Society."

"His name?"

"Dr Martín Honores. He lives at twenty-seven Calle Arenales."

"Good, carry on."

"I came across señor Soler in the lobby. My first impression was that he was unwell. He told me what had happened."

"How did you find the victim?"

"In the same position as she is now."

"You didn't move her?"

"I simply examined her. I don't believe I moved her."

"Do you know her?"

Luchter's face, which normally had the healthy glow of a man who practises plenty of outdoor sport, was pale. Without even casting a glance towards where she lay, he declared he did not know the person in the lift.

"Was it you who called the police?"

"Yes, I called from my apartment. Señor Soler was with me. We went up together to notify the caretaker."

"So you're telling me everything is as you found it."

"That's correct."

"But señor Soler has said you opened the deceased's handbag."

"That's true. I wanted to see if there was anything that might indicate who she was and whether she lived in this building. To save time, I mean."

"Poor move."

Luchter silently agreed. Authority is like the word of God, difficult to dispute if one feels its presence.

"So it's true that the young woman's lipstick fell into the lift shaft?"

"Yes, it is."

The Superintendent turned to Vera, who had just entered the lobby.

"As soon as the body has been removed, have one of the officers go down with the caretaker. We need to retrieve a lipstick that fell down there."

He pointed to the lift shaft. His gaze then travelled restlessly over everyone present.

"Which of you is the caretaker?"

Andrés and Aurora Torres stepped forward together like the inseparable stars of a constellation. At last, the identification!

Aurora was sniffing at clues in her memory. Andrés shook his head. He did not recognize the elegant figure. Aurora saw a topaz-coloured jersey dress under the fur coat and beautiful, dark suede stilettos. The woman's long blond hair fell languidly, framing sharp features that when still alive must have given her an air of impertinence, and which death made sharper still.

"I've never seen her," declared Torres.

A joyful yelp from Aurora undermined his resounding conviction.

"Well, I do think I've seen her. I met her in the lift when I was going down to clean the first floor."

Torres's withering look reached Aurora at the same time as the Superintendent's question.

"Had you seen her before that?"

"No, sir, no." Aurora now took refuge in the single sighting as a mitigation of possible complications. "Just once! It was last week and she was dressed just as she is now. That's how I remembered her, nothing else."

"Where was she going? To which floor?"

Aurora chose not to look at her husband.

"She said she was going to the ground floor and that I'd made her go up unnecessarily when she took the lift. As if I give people rides for fun!"

"Tell me everyone who lives in the building," the Superintendent said to Torres.

"On the first floor it's the Suárez Loza family, who are away in Europe at the moment. On the second floor, señor Iñarra and his family; on the third, señor Czerbó and his sister; on the fourth, señor Soler; on the fifth, Dr Luchter. Everyone here is very peaceful, señor Superintendent."

The same old story. It was just what Superintendent Lahore expected: peaceful buildings and good people, always the same. So how was it possible that so much went on?

"We must call all those who aren't yet here. Someone has to identify the body. She must be a friend or acquaintance of one of the residents."

One of the police officers went upstairs with Torres. Soler was dozing on the sofa. Everyone else eyed one another in silence. Officer Vera was writing in his small notebook. Aurora had adopted a spiteful, curious expression that revealed the breadth of her inner world.

Two more women soon appeared. The first, who looked no older than thirty-five, was wearing a comfortable dark red dressing gown and slippers of the same colour. She was dark-skinned and slight. She wore no make-up so the yellowish tone of her olive skin and the two grooves at either side of her mouth were clearly visible. Her dark eyes had metallic glints. The other was a girl of no more than twenty, tall and pleasant-looking, with a round face and the kind of nose that twitches and gives its owner a mocking air. She was dressed for going out, in a black skirt and a bright green cashmere top.

"My husband can't come down, Superintendent," explained the older woman to Lahore. "I've already told the officer that he isn't well. Dr Luchter can testify to that, my husband is his patient."

"That's correct," Luchter hurriedly confirmed, "señor Iñarra suffers from a nervous condition. He should not be disturbed unless absolutely necessary."

"We're not planning on disturbing any of you. All we want is for you to identify this person."

The two women examined the body with swift glances, then said they'd never seen the victim before.

"Good evening," called a bright voice from outside. Superintendent Lahore frowned at Vera.

"I told you to call Inspector Ericourt."

"He wasn't there. Blasi answered the call."

This same Blasi joined the group, followed by several photographers.

"Are they journalists?"

Señora de Iñarra's voice trembled as she asked the question. No one answered her.

The photographers were already focusing on the body in the lift. Soler sat up when he heard the first flash, muttering something about letting a person sleep in peace. Señora de Iñarra turned towards Luchter.

"Please don't let them photograph us. It would be horrible to appear in the papers."

"This is Inspector Ericourt's secretary, madam," explained Officer Vera. "The photos are for the police record."

Meanwhile another two people had appeared, accompanied this time by the Officer and Andrés. A tall, thin, dark-skinned man with pronounced cheekbones and a woman with washed-out hair and a harried look. Both were wearing scruffy stay-at-home clothes.

The man introduced himself as Boris Czerbó, Bulgarian, resident in Argentina for two years. He explained that the woman was his sister Rita. Too afraid to speak, she simply nodded when she heard her name.

The police procedures were starting in earnest outside. An ambulance had stopped next to the cordon on the pavement and on the other side of the door were the restless, wide-awake

19

faces of newspaper reporters. Señora de Iñarra spoke to the Superintendent; her graceful Madrid accent lent her question a feminine touch.

"Is our presence absolutely necessary, sir? I've left my husband in the care of the maid."

"No, madam, you can go. But please understand that you must not leave your home until authorized to do so."

Beatriz Iñarra, sitting next to Soler, bit her nails and periodically shrugged her shoulders to shake off the drunken man who persisted in leaning against her chest.

"I'll stay, Gabriela," she announced. "This is more fun than sitting in my room, reading."

Each of the words sounded as definitive as if it were followed by a full stop.

The only commentary was an approving smile from Blasi, seen by no one because it was directed at his shoes. Dr Luchter took señora de Iñarra's arm.

"I'll go with you, madam, if you don't mind."

There was silence once they had both left, as well as a sense that something was going to happen. And indeed, a few seconds later Czerbó spoke, mangling the words with his terrible accent and even worse grasp of Spanish syntax:

"Señor Superintendent, you ask me if I am know the lady. She Frida Eidinger. I know husband. Lives Villa Devoto, Calle Lácar forty-one."

Vera grabbed his notebook. The others feigned indifference. A snore from Soler broke the monotonous tension. Lahore weighed up the sleeping man with desperation.

"Was this woman a guest in your home this evening?" he asked Czerbó.

"No, mister. She not guest of us."

The voice had become sickly sweet.

"So then, how do you know her?"

Behind Boris Czerbó, Rita's face was red with shock.

"Her husband is client of me."

"And how do you explain señora Eidinger's presence here?"

All eyes focused on Czerbó. He let his arms fall wearily.

"I cannot explain nothing."

"Where were you at the time señora Eidinger died?"

"Can you tell me in what time this happened?"

He smiled with a cynic's empty grimace. The cheerful glimmer faded from Lahore's eyes and, calling aside the doctor who had come with the ambulance and certified the body, he exchanged a few words with him. He then turned back to face Czerbó.

"She died at approximately one thirty, or rather between one thirty and two in the morning, from poisoning," he said.

"In that time I slept," replied Czerbó, unruffled.

His sister confirmed his words with another nod.

"Who else lives with you?"

"No one. We not having servants."

"Very well."

Lahore stepped aside to make way for the stretcher bearing Frida Eidinger's body. Rita and señorita Iñarra averted their eyes. Soler, who had woken up and was about to light a cigarette, threw it to the floor with a repulsed grimace. Frida Eidinger was leaving the scene of her death accompanied only by disgust.

Only Aurora Torres seemed curious and craned her neck to watch how the stretcher-bearers loaded the body into the ambulance.

"Dear goodness!" she exclaimed, distractedly crossing herself.

21

"You're all free to go," Lahore said to everyone present, "I'll call if I need you."

They filed towards the service lift in silence. As the ambulance's siren tore through the air the lobby filled with palpable worry and mistrust. The empty lift, its light still on, opened its jaws to suspicion. Lahore moved away quickly, shaking off the journalists who were trying to besiege him.

An hour later, Blasi was knocking on the door of Soler's apartment. After a few minutes Soler appeared holding a bag of ice to his head. When he recognized the Inspector's secretary his face became one of consternation.

"It's you! Have you come for me?"

"Not yet. This is a social visit. May I come in?"

"Of course, I was just making a cup of coffee. My head's spinning."

The harmonious combination of antique furniture and modern details in Soler's apartment revealed the care with which those educated in good taste and a profound sense of elegance always decorate a house. From the door one could sense the comfort of the place. Blasi breathed it in like a lungful of fresh air.

"What can they want with me now?" asked Soler. "I don't know who she was."

"She was Frida Eidinger," said Blasi, "just as that brute with the frightful Spanish said. I was in the morgue when her husband identified the body."

Water was bubbling in the coffee percolator. Dark liquid thickened in the upper glass bowl as the gurgling column of boiling water rose towards the filter. Soler, frowning, put the cap on the alcohol burner.

"An instinctive gesture, covering up," thought Blasi, who had acquired certain psychological assumptions and was keen to get rid of them through practical application.

"Then I swear I don't know what they want with me," said Soler.

"They assume you were with her."

"But I didn't know her! I've told the truth and I can prove it. I was seen in a nightclub with a girl a few minutes before I came back here. My companion will tell you that I escorted her home."

"And if she doesn't?"

Soler simultaneously considered the sugar bowl and this absurd possibility. His thoughts must have led him to an optimistic conclusion because he smiled as he offered Blasi a cup of coffee.

"Luisita wouldn't do that to me."

"Suppose she went out with you, shall we say, unofficially. It must happen a lot with the kind of relationships you seem to cultivate."

Soler drank the bitter coffee in one gulp.

"Not with her, she's a loyal girl."

"Don't kid yourself. The loyalty of girls like her shifts like a weathervane."

"What are you suggesting? Do you mean to help me?"

In Soler's moral code, teasing naturally meant mistrust.

"Aren't you from the police?"

"That's exactly the point. I aim to save time and I believe pursuing you would mean wasting it, which is why I came to see you. I'd like you to tell me what you can about the others."

"Do you really take me for a gossip?"

"No, for someone who lives in the same building. Everyone has something to say, even if it is only general observations.

What do you do when you're standing in front of a painting?
You adopt different positions until you get the best perspective. Do you see?"

"Not entirely." Soler poured himself another cup of coffee.
"Nor do I see why a suicide has to be so complicated."

"Do you really think the lift in an apartment building is
where a stranger would choose to commit suicide? The police
are assuming someone put the body there. But who?"

His inquisitive smile surprised Soler.

"It wasn't me," he said.

"OK, it wasn't you. So tell me about the others. Who are
they?"

Soler let out a sigh in surrender.

"Who do you want me to start with? This job isn't for me. I
don't know how to do it."

"Let's eliminate Luchter because he wasn't at home. That
leaves the Iñarras. Is señor Iñarra as unwell as his wife says
he is?"

"Señor Iñarra is a respectable person. The whole family is."

Blasi had naturally discounted Soler's partiality. Groups
form as soon as danger rears its head.

"His wife looks too young to be the mother of that girl.
What's her name?"

"Betty, I mean Beatriz. Señora de Iñarra is her stepmother."
Soler paused. "You'll find out in any case. She was Betty's nursemaid when her mother was alive. She married señor Iñarra not
long after he was widowed, and ever since then she's dedicated
her life to him," he added, using the idea of sacrifice to explain
a marriage he must have thought unequal. "Betty's very independent, she's not at home much."

"Caramba! How do you know that?"

Soler pointed sheepishly towards the light shaft window.

"And the others?"

"The Czerbós? They haven't lived here long and they're a real mystery. I shouldn't tell you anything. It's not my place."

A man holding a bag of ice to his head and gulping down large cups of coffee becomes a caricature when he starts outlining his moral obligations. Blasi carried on regardless.

"The sister seems very intimidated."

"She's always like that. She works like a slave for him, even though people say he's a rich man."

"They're Bulgarian?"

"They used to live in Germany. They came over soon after the war ended."

The doorbell interrupted them.

"I'll answer it," said Blasi, standing up. "Go and get dressed."

Vera was at the door with two other officers. Blasi looked sidelong into the apartment. Soler had disappeared.

"Are you making an arrest?"

"Not yet, but there's a serious charge. Are you coming with us?"

Blasi shook his head.

"I haven't finished my rounds. My boss is getting me to work on my social skills. I have to go up to the caretaker's apartment."

Gabriela de Iñarra entered the bedroom carrying a steaming cup of tea on a tray, which she put down on the bedside table. Don Agustín's left arm trembled constantly on top of the blankets and although his face, aged by his illness, was stern, he spoke to his wife in a sweet, measured voice.

"Thank you, darling. You always go to such trouble. You're an angel."

Betty Iñarra was reading a magazine in the corner of the room. Hearing her father's words, she buried her nose in the pages.

"Your heart rate is fine, Don Agustín," said Dr Luchter. He was standing next to the bed, preparing a syringe. The bedside lamp cast a circle of white light over the scene.

"I feel absolutely fine," said his patient. "Sleepless nights are old acquaintances of mine. They don't affect me. It's young people who need their sleep."

Iñarra's eyes sought his daughter.

"Did you get dressed to go out, darling?"

"I didn't get dressed," Betty replied, imitating her father's measured tone. "I was dressed when they called me."

Gabriela threw her stepdaughter a pleading look.

"She shouldn't humiliate him like that," she whispered to Dr Luchter. He lowered his eyes to better observe the transfer of liquid from the vial to the syringe.

"You went out earlier, then?" asked Don Agustín.

"I went to the cinema with Raquel."

"And you're still dressed at three in the morning?"

His voice communicated cold disapproval.

"You know I don't like you going out alone at night. Gabriela, why didn't you tell me Betty had gone out?"

He had called her Gabriela, not Gaby. The voice of reproach.

"It's not easy to tell Betty what to do," said Gabriela apologetically.

Dr Luchter leant over his patient. His furrowed brow added years to his rosy face.

26

"I don't blame you, dear. I'm just telling you what's best for you both. I'm responsible for keeping you safe. You and Betty both know you can always count on my protection."

"You've protected me so much, Dad, I've had enough!" Betty said irreverently. "Save your protection for Gabriela, she needs it more than me."

"The alcohol, please," Luchter asked Gabriela. She looked for it on the side table. Her eyes had filled with tears she was struggling to hold back.

The telephone suddenly rang in the living room. Betty leapt up. She returned to the bedroom a few seconds later.

"It's for you, Doctor," she said with forced indifference. The doctor and the girl exchanged a look of mutual understanding.

It was Superintendent Lahore, wanting to see Dr Luchter. He said he had called his apartment to no avail and thought he would find him with his patient. Luchter promised to drop by the station at once.

His work with the Iñarras was done. Don Augustín's condition was satisfactory and the unusual events did not seem to have affected him. It made sense. Sick people wrap themselves up in their own concerns and become entirely indifferent to the outside world. Their rooms are cells separated from the social hive. Their walls get thicker and end up as impenetrable as the shell of a snail.

At the station, Luchter found Lahore waiting for him in his office.

"Look, Doctor," Lahore said to him, "I wanted to see you because I'd like you to recall the details as precisely as possible. According to your statement, you opened señora Eidinger's handbag in search of something that would identify her."

"That is correct."

"And according to what Soler has said, as you did so the contents of the handbag fell to the floor and the lipstick disappeared down the gap by the lift door."

"Exactly."

"Do you remember if anything else fell out of the handbag at the same time?"

"I don't believe so."

The Superintendent looked at him with irritation.

"You don't believe so? Can't you be sure?"

"I didn't see anything else. I can't be sure of anything but that."

"That tallies with what Soler says. But look."

Carefully and professionally, he picked up a key ring that was on his desk.

"Señor Eidinger identified this key ring as belonging to his wife. On it is a key to the main door of your building. Do you know what that means?"

"More or less," admitted the doctor modestly.

"It means that someone has lied. This key means that the victim had been to visit someone she knew well. It means she was in the habit of visiting the building at hours when her presence there would go unnoticed, it means someone got rid of the key ring because they thought it would be compromising. Can we therefore consider this a case of simple suicide?"

"Don't ask me," was what Luchter's dismissive gesture seemed to say.

"I didn't know señora Eidinger, and I can prove where I was that night," he explained.

"I know that," said the Superintendent, shuffling some papers, "I have Dr Honores's statement here. You left his house at two a.m.

and went straight to the garage where you usually keep your car. The night watchman and the valet saw you enter at ten past two, therefore you took no more time than strictly necessary to make the journey. Your situation is clear."

"And so?" asked Luchter's eyebrows, arched like circumflex accents.

Superintendent Lahore leaned forward. His round, dark face bore a good-natured expression that seemed to say, "Come on, you can tell Daddy."

"Do you think Soler was telling the truth?"

He immediately understood that he'd made a mistake. Luchter was a discreet man and pseudo-camaraderie irritated him.

"He was very drunk. *In vino veritas*," said the doctor.

"Yes, yes, of course, but you found him alone with the body, isn't that right?"

"He told me he had just arrived."

"That's what he claims. He won't be dragged away from that, as it were."

Those simple words hid a depth of troubling questions, with one—the essential one—coming and going like the theme of a symphony. Soler did not inspire pity in Luchter. He felt no compassion towards him.

"I don't think he's lying," he added all the same. He had believed what Soler said since the outset.

"All the same, there is no doubt that señora Eidinger went to the building to see someone."

"Of course."

"Who threw the key ring away? Her?"

Luchter remained silent.

"May I ask you something, Superintendent?" he said at last.

Lahore nodded.

"I suppose you'll interrogate all the building's residents again, won't you? As a doctor I would ask you to please not disturb my patient, señor Iñarra. He suffers from a nervous disorder that affects his mobility and can, to all intents and purposes, be considered disabled. As far as possible, interrogate him in his home."

"What does he suffer from?"

"A disease of the spinal cord. His left arm and leg are affected by a continuous tremor. He never leaves his home."

"We'll bear that in mind," the Superintendent assured him. He seemed an amiable man who was satisfied by the rare opportunity for kindness.

"As for me," Luchter went on, "I'm happy to help. I'll leave you my number at the hospital so you can call if you need me during the morning." As he spoke, Luchter took out his pen with the methodical flourish of someone accustomed to adding touches of ceremony to the most insignificant gestures.

Lahore accompanied him to the office door. The police station was a few blocks from his building and Luchter slowly made his way home. He walked with his fists closed tight inside the pockets of his overcoat and his eyes fixed on the ground.

A police officer was watching the front door and the main lift was out of service. Luchter went up in the service lift and tiptoed into his apartment so as not to wake the cook. It was almost six a.m.

The light of the August morning was beginning to make its presence felt in the dark apartment like an invisible hand fraying the silent domestic shadows. Luchter went over to the drinks cabinet and poured himself a glass of whisky, then sat down in one of the armchairs and rested his head back. His closed eyes gave his face the immobile quality of a plaster mask. He sat up to bring the glass to his lips, but a sudden grimace of repulsion stopped the movement short. Little by little his features relaxed and his whole face took on an expression of infinite sadness.

Gabriela de Iñarra arranged her husband's pillows and pulled the covers up until they almost covered his chin. Then, leaning over, she kissed him goodnight on the forehead.

"Try to get some sleep, darling," Don Agustín said to her. "This business must have made you very nervous."

"Only for your sake. You must rest now. It's silly for us to worry. It's nothing to do with us, after all."

"Don't fret over me. You make me feel like a burden. You don't have to sacrifice yourself for me."

The softness of his voice didn't temper the severity of his gaze or his hard-set mouth. Gabriela turned pale, as if he had just threatened to hit her.

"Agustín, why do you say that? I don't like it when you say things like that. I look after you because I want to, and sometimes it seems you're determined to remind me of what I've long forgotten."

Iñarra reached for his wife's hand, which she had retracted so it now hung at her side.

"For God's sake, Gaby! Why do you always get the wrong idea? I must have put it badly. Your constant goodwill makes me feel as though you're not entirely sincere."

Gabriela pulled away from the hand, which had settled for clutching the folds of her apron.

"Doubts make nasty enemies," she said decisively. "Try to get some sleep, Agustín."

She walked to the door with her head bent low. From there she turned to add, in a simpler tone:

31

"I'd feel better if you could just accept things naturally. Good-night, Agustín."

As she passed the door to Betty's room, Gabriela stopped. Betty was walking around the room. She was surely getting undressed for bed. She heard the sound of a body reclining, then a metallic click. Yes, there was no doubt. Betty had just picked up the telephone receiver and was dialling a number.

She held her breath and leant against the door to hear better. The hall stretched out in front of her like a dark stain split by the sliver of light coming from under Betty's door.

"Hello," she said, "are you alone?"

A silence.

"Don't say anything. It's better that way."

Another silence.

"Yes, yes, see you tomorrow."

Gaby heard the click of the receiver being replaced on the stand, then she moved away silently. Once she was in her bedroom and had got into bed, she took a packet of cigarettes from the drawer in her bedside table. Long hours unfurled ahead of her like an image multiplied in a house of mirrors. She smoked with relish, tricking her wakeful anxiety with the calm appearance of her gestures, her gaze lost in the whitish smoke that slowly dissipated in the darkness of the room.

Boris Czerbó said goodbye to Blasi at the door to his apartment. The innocuous questions had sapped his spirits and left in his mouth the bitter taste of the past being churned up. Behind him Rita waited, ingenuous and terrified, her expression of total submission inciting him to cruelty and spite.

"Don't just stand there," he said in their native language. "Go and check everything's ready for me. I'll need two tablets to sleep tonight."

Rita had picked up an ashtray to empty but her hands were trembling so much that she dropped it. Cigarette butts rolled onto the carpet and Rita stared in fright at where the ash now blurred a patch of the Persian design.

"Clumsy cow," Boris muttered. "You're a waste of space. Always have been."

Rita burst into tears. Boris pursed his lips in annoyance.

"Clean that up before you go to bed. Goodnight."

But Rita's presence followed him to his bedroom, which was full of her preparations: two glasses, one containing water and one with some black prunes floating inside. The brownish liquid testified to the fact that they had been put there some time ago. Next to the glasses he saw the tube of sleeping tablets and a packet of cigarettes. Everything was in order.

He heard Rita's footsteps in the living room. Lulled by the familiar sound, a pleasant drowsiness gradually crept over Boris. Very soon "that thing" started to rear its head. A series of scenes paraded before his bleary eyes. The cage doors opened to make way for dark memories of a certain time. Rita loomed up, with her resigned and soulless presence.

"She will never know peace, ever," Boris said to himself.

The cabalistic phrase soon dissolved the fearsome images. Sleep closed the doors of consciousness. Boris felt the knot in his chest loosening and, giving way to the sensation of well-being, he let himself be carried off by a stupor that rocked him like waves on a beach.

2

The Moon in the Window

That afternoon, at siesta time, the plaza of Villa Devoto looked like a peaceful village square. Local women were knitting and chatting under the huge eucalyptus trees. Every now and then a child ran up to one of them before trotting off, proudly jangling the coveted prize in his or her hand: a few coins for the chocolate seller or the merry-go-round.

Three people were sitting on one of the benches. A man was reading the crime pages of the morning paper with his hat pulled down over his eyes. The two women next to him eyed him askance, apparently absorbed in counting the stitches of their knitting. The man soon began to nod off over the journalistic suppositions, and when the newspaper fell to his feet he made no move to recover it. The women raised their eyes. His head dropped onto his chest, with the indiscretion common to those who sleep in public places.

One of the women then pointed the toe of her shoe towards a headline in the crime pages.

"Poor Frida," she sighed.

Her companion glanced about before bending to pick up the newspaper. The children were playing at least twenty paces from the bench. She folded the paper and placed it next to the sleeping man, allowing herself time to skim through the report she already knew by heart.

"I don't feel sorry for her," she said. "She was a stranger. I never liked her."

"No, don't say that." The other woman seemed less susceptible to prejudice and thus more open to compassion. "Eidinger wasn't a stranger. His family has lived around here since he was the age our kids are now."

"What does that have to do with it?

They spoke in hushed tones, with the lukewarm conviction of aspirational gossips.

"He married so mysteriously. No one knows who she was."

"A girl from a nice family."

"A girl from a rich family. I suppose that must've been a factor in their love at first sight. Heiresses always believe they're making conquests. My husband reminded me of that this morning. He never trusted Frida Eidinger."

Male opinion muscled into the conversation.

"But do you know anything?"

"No, no, nothing. No one has really been able to say anything about Frida Eidinger. Tell me the truth, would you have made friends with her all the same?"

"Frida wasn't looking for our friendship." The sincere remark sounded like a posthumous homage.

"She might not have been. Eidinger, on the other hand, often came to the pharmacy to talk to my husband. I think he was trying to get an invitation for himself and his wife to our house. My husband pretended not to cotton on, of course, but he had no choice but to accept an invitation to theirs one Saturday afternoon."

"Oh, really? You never told me that."

The fierce irony in that comment was the verbal equivalent of a dressmaker's pincushion.

"Of course I regretted having accepted the invitation," said the woman, continuing her story. "They'd asked us to go early so we'd have time to play a game of canasta after tea. Gustavo came out to meet us."

"People say their house was very nicely done out."

"Oh, yes. He spent his last pesos on it before she came over from Europe. Well, as I was saying, Frida didn't appear and Gustavo hurriedly said she'd be a little late because she'd been busy in the kitchen until the last minute getting the tea ready."

"She was very clever, wasn't she?"

"Pf... just like the rest of them, except she spent money without a second thought. It's easy to be clever like that. Well, at the end of the day it was *her* money. A quarter of an hour went by and Frida still hadn't appeared. Gustavo went up to go and find her. We waited a good while. We could hear them talking upstairs."

"They were shouting that loudly? Weren't you in the living room?"

The storyteller blushed slightly.

"Gustavo had left the door open and their voices carried down to us. Of course there was no indiscretion on our part because they were speaking German so we didn't understand anything they were saying. Suddenly Gustavo rushed down all flustered and went out, slamming the door without saying goodbye. Shortly afterwards Frida came in looking very calm, saying that Gustavo had had to go out but would be back soon. She insisted we take our tea without waiting for him. You can imagine how uncomfortable we felt."

"And Frida?"

"Unruffled. She was adamant that we should play cards. I made it clear to my husband that if Gustavo came back the situation would get very tense, so we left. We didn't return the invitation, of course."

A little girl ran up and buried her tearful face in the story-teller's skirts.

"Chiche, I don't like you telling tales," the mother reprimanded loudly. The sleeping man had opened his eyes and was watching the scene with a glazed look. A second later, his eyelids drooped involuntarily.

The other woman looked at her watch and put her knitting away in a cloth bag.

"Four o'clock! Where can those kids be?" she exclaimed as she stood up. "Are you staying here?"

"No, no, I'll come with you."

They left, with the mother dragging the weeping girl along. The man settled himself more comfortably on the bench, with no apparent intention of interrupting his siesta. He was not alone for long. A bright, friendly looking young man approached along the eucalyptus-lined street. He was not wearing a hat and the wind lifted his brown hair. He joined the other man on the bench.

"Did they take the bait?" the sleeping man muttered between his teeth.

The young man shook his head.

"How about here?" he asked, pointing at the bench.

"Somewhat. The human benevolence of boredom," said Superintendent Inspector Santiago Ericourt to his assistant Ferruccio Blasi.

Ericourt was a corpulent man from whose wide face protruded an aquiline nose and a square chin. When not speaking, the outline of his features gave him an air of unwillingness and distraction that others easily took for rejection, as if he were ill disposed towards friendliness. However, the watchful look in his brown eyes denoted something more than an inquisitive drive to close cases. He could spend days following the lead of a name, hiding his agitation behind an innocuous screen of abstraction. He had nothing of the prowling predator, but all the fearsome patience of an elephant scanning the ground with its trunk for the piece of food it has dropped.

When discussing his fellow men he seemed animated by the goodwill of those to whom the Kingdom of Heaven has been promised, but he pursued them all the same. For him, in a way, justice and truth took on the nature of a sporting tournament whose interest is renewed every day. Blasi admired how he remained permanently alert under his outward appearance of lethargy.

"Eidinger is expecting us now," said Ericourt. "I told him we were coming. He seemed very happy to see us."

"I met him in the morgue the night before last. He gives the impression of a good fellow overly concerned by what others think."

"We've got nothing on him, Blasi. When they went to find him he'd just got back from a Photography Club meeting. At least ten people testified that he didn't leave the place all night. They were holding an AGM."

The afternoon winter sun projected a few warm rays that caressed them like long fingers, creating an atmosphere that inspired trust.

"Frida Eidinger," Ericourt went on in his measured tone, "must have planned her suicide as a revenge. That's why she chose the lift, because it was the best way to put the man she wanted to hurt in an awkward position: a partial incrimination that would open the doors to the most dangerous hypotheses."

"But why does it necessarily have to be suicide?" Blasi objected, angry with himself for thinking how nice it would be to sit in that square with no other motive than to soak up the sun, disconsolately bored by the lack of anything to do.

Ericourt took off his hat and twirled it between his spatulate fingers.

"I don't believe it was suicide either. But we have to admit it as a possibility. Frida Eidinger might have gone to the house to see one of three men: Luchter, Czerbó or Soler. For reasons of good taste we'll discount Iñarra. Czerbó was the only one in his apartment. How do we prove she went to see him? All their statements are logical and do not contradict one another. There is a grey area, but not surrounding Czerbó."

"Who then?" asked Blasi.

"It's strange that if señorita Iñarra returned home between one thirty and two, as she claims, she didn't come across the victim in the lift."

"She says she took the stairs."

"After having walked her cousin home and then back to her own building. In that case the girl is obsessed with physical exercise."

"I don't like clues," Blasi contended. "Their interpretation often leads us the wrong way."

Ericourt stood up. The two men walked in silence along the wide path flanked by trees whose bark split open to reveal the pale, fleshy insides of their trunks, strong as columns. The wind shook the branches, covering the ground with the small red filaments of their flowers. The soft afternoon air was filled with the scent of eucalyptus. Blasi became engrossed in the childish task of treading on the arabesques of sun and shade.

"Last night," Ericourt said in the emphatically recitative tone he used when putting his ideas in order, "I was working at home until late. I needed to look over some files. My desk is in front of the window. The night was starry and if I had to classify it, I would say it was a moonless winter night. A good while went by; when I looked up again, a waning moon hung in the centre of the window frame. For hours I had considered it inexistent because it was invisible to me. So you see how the evidence of a fact is purely a question of perspective."

Blasi was still absorbed in his infantile game with the patches of sun.

"There is always a truth, even if it's hidden," Ericourt went on, "but the facts inexorably describe their orbit and at a certain point a piece of evidence appears before us with the same clarity as the waning moon that appeared to me last night. Sometimes we have to wait, sometimes the truth reveals itself unexpectedly."

"I'd like to think it was suicide," said Blasi. "That's the most logical. Lahore is sure of it."

"It is the most logical. But logic has the inherent defect of being personal."

"According to Lahore, señora Eidinger was a friend of Soler's and had been to visit him that night. Soler had given her a key to the main door but not his flat so as to avoid problems because he leads a, shall we say, carefree life. Not finding him at home, she left. When she got to the lobby she met him arriving home at that very moment. There had been jealousy between them and threats to end the relationship. They surely had a vicious argument and she ingested the cyanide."

"How? Where was she carrying it? Let's suppose she had it in a capsule. Did Soler get her a glass of water so she could take it?"

"She might have had it in a paper wrapper, just as they prepare powders in a pharmacy. All you have to do is put it on your tongue for it to take effect."

"Do you believe that's what happened?"

"It's not in Soler's nature to drive a woman crazy enough to take her own life. He's too superficial."

"We must accept that there are women who don't need any encouragement to stir up an atmosphere of tragedy."

They had crossed the avenue and were walking along a quiet, sunny suburban street between two rows of small houses whose windows were all shut fast. The homes of the discreet middle class.

"There are the others," said Ericourt, "who, like anyone involved in strange events, seem curious. But let's not get ideas. A bit of limelight turns simple faults that common people easily forgive in one another into monstrous anomalies. Luchter is a hard-working and meticulous man, with no known vices. He's lived in the apartment for three years and set up his surgery there. Frida Eidinger is not one of his patients. His nurse didn't know her. He has fought hard to get where he is now, having travelled from Germany as a legitimate immigrant just before the start of the war. As for the Czerbós, general opinion pities Rita, who is subject to her brother's despotism and miserliness. He came to Argentina in 1946, she followed him in 1947. Boris was a photographer in Hamburg until 1944. The Iñarras are the longest-standing residents along with Soler. They lived there when Don Agustín's first wife was alive. Aurora Torres takes pleasure in telling the story of his second marriage to his daughter's nursemaid…"

Ericourt had stopped outside a pretty, English-style house, set back from the pavement, behind a small garden.

"According to the caretakers," cut in Blasi, "Don Agustín is one of those men who intoxicate themselves with charity so as to spread their beneficent wings over those around them."

"Don't be so prejudiced against charity. This is Eidinger's house," said Ericourt, interrupting him.

3

A Home and a Victim

The man who answered the door was tall and smartly dressed. His curly brown hair was beginning to thin at the temples, announcing a maturity that his slim figure would belie for many years yet. A wide mouth and sharp nose between small eyes lent his face an anxious, rat-like mobility.

As he greeted the police officers, whose visit he had been expecting, Gustavo Eidinger showed more insecurity than hostility or mistrust. His wife's mysterious death had put him in the difficult situation of having to carry out his husbandly duties and face the malevolent curiosity of neighbours, without a verdict that might clarify whether or not she had wronged him. He was a man given over to the torturous conflict of doubt.

His furtive looks and nervous gestures (he was chewing the end of an unlit pipe that he passed repeatedly from one hand to the other) betrayed his unease. Santiago Ericourt, accepting his invitation, entered the small living room with Blasi behind him. The house had not lost the smart, impersonal coldness of a place only recently decorated. Perhaps the sole touch of warmth was provided by the photographs that stood on a side table, one of sunlight on branches and the other of Frida in Tyrolean dress.

Gustavo Eidinger was closely following Ericourt's roaming gaze when he noticed it coming to rest on the photo of his wife. Then he broke the silence that had settled over him and his guests since his words of greeting and invitation to enter the living room.

"They've promised to hand the body over to me tomorrow. I've decided that the funeral will be a private affair straight from the morgue."

A wise plan. Any ceremony would be difficult to handle. He tried to speak naturally but his subdued tone slipped into one of humiliation.

"It'll be a while longer before they return the personal items from the laboratory," said Ericourt.

"I know. I'd like to have all this over with as soon as possible. I've been thinking about going away."

"Good idea."

Gustavo's words revealed his overwhelming need to talk about Frida. Reluctant to stray from his memories, he sought to prolong her existence by constantly inserting her name into the conversation. The silence stretched out once more into minutes of reticent expectation, a silence between people attempting to set the course of a conversation.

"So how can I help you?" Eidinger said at last, offering them cigarettes.

"You'll soon see more or less why we've come," said the Superintendent. "I'm after some personal information that need not feature in the official investigation."

"I've already told you everything I know about my wife. I don't think I can add much more." Eidinger was not avoiding his gaze, but he was not helping the situation with his feigned calm, either.

"There are, however, certain things that you can perhaps help us understand better," Ericourt insisted.

"Such as?"

"Such as your state of mind on the night of the 23rd of August when you arrived home and didn't find your wife waiting for you."

Eidinger held up the palms of his hands.

"What could I do? I waited for Frida to come back so she could explain why she'd gone out at such an ungodly hour."

"Very reasonable," said Ericourt approvingly, "but had anything like that happened before?"

"Never," Eidinger answered hurriedly. "At least as far as I knew."

"Did you often go out at night?"

Eidinger hesitated.

"To the Club once or twice a week."

"You never supposed that your wife might go out too?"

"She was always at home when I got back." Caught off-guard, he sounded sincere.

"Was your relationship with your wife affectionate, of late?"

Eidinger answered like a docile lad who folds under the weight of insinuations.

"We'd had some arguments but not what I'd call serious ones. Frida's character was as impulsive as mine."

"You hadn't been married for very long, am I right?"

"About a year and a half."

Ericourt half closed his eyes as if trying to remember something.

"You married in Germany."

"We married by proxy," Eidinger corrected him, "I met Frida in Zurich. She'd been living there since the end of the war. Frida was orphaned very young and spent periods with different relatives. She didn't have a fixed address."

"Yours wasn't a long engagement, then."

"No," Eidinger admitted, somewhat embarrassed. "We hardly had time to get to know one another. Frida accepted my marriage proposal straight away—" He stopped himself and scrutinized his visitors' faces, fearing his words might make him appear smug. "She was very eager to leave Europe," he said by way of explanation.

"Oh, yes? And why was that?"

Eidinger looked at him in surprise. Did he really have to spell out something so simple?

"She was afraid of another war. Like so many others she felt deeply wounded by what they'd just gone through."

"Why didn't you marry before you came back, then?"

"We arranged that I would return to Buenos Aires first to get the house ready. Frida preferred it that way. In her letters she told me she'd travel over as soon as possible. I must confess I sought that brief separation as a test."

"Do you still have the letters?"

Gustavo seemed offended.

"Of course. Frida kept them in her desk."

Really? How strange. You don't give love letters back unless the relationship has ended. Why had she kept them instead of him? It was time for the thorny question.

"Was yours a happy marriage, señor Eidinger?"

His pause answered better than words. Happiness admits no doubt.

"Well, deep down, yes, but daily life, you know…"

"So, in other words, it was not."

Eidinger retreated in search of solid support for his married life.

"That's not what I meant to say. Don't get me wrong. Frida and I didn't know each other well. We had to get used to one another after we married, and we didn't have long," he concluded painfully.

He had abandoned the good-natured attitude of earlier in their conversation and was now a man ready to bristle bad-temperedly in defence of his private life. This made him easier to attack.

"How old was your wife, señor Eidinger?"

"Thirty-two."

"At that age a woman has a past. What can you tell us about that?"

"Frida was very discreet," the widower said, poking at the tobacco in his unlit pipe. "She didn't talk about herself."

The living room door creaked slightly. In poked the whiskery, rectangular head of a fox terrier. The animal ran to Ericourt's feet and began to lick his shoes.

"Stop that, Muck!" Eidinger ordered. The dog raised its snout and ears then went back to doing just the same.

"He's Frida's dog," Eidinger explained. "He does that to anyone he sees for the first time."

Ericourt had stood up. Blasi patted the animal's back affectionately.

"Could you show us the letters you mentioned, señor Eidinger?"

"Of course. They're in Frida's bedroom. Would you like to go with me or should I bring them down?"

"We'll follow you." Ericourt shot a sidelong look at Blasi.

The pretentious decor of señora Eidinger's bedroom contrasted with the rest of the house. As if he ought to apologize for things that were not his responsibility, Eidinger explained that his wife had insisted on decorating the room that way. The walls were hung with finely striped, black-and-white paper. The furniture was made from white sycamore and the bed, a wide divan pushed against one of the walls, had a black satin cover. The dressing table was a simple stand under a rectangular mirror, and on it, carefully arranged, were an ivory-handled manicure set and a matching powder compact, eau de Cologne bottles and a lipstick case all made from glass and black enamel.

On two small bedside tables stood a pair of standard lamps with white parchment shades, the bases of which were female torsos sculpted in ebony. The room's centrepiece, however, given its size and colour, was a picture of the zodiac symbol for Scorpio that hung above the bed.

Muck had followed them, and was rushing from one side to another looking for the presence that caused currents of cold and sorrow to circulate around the room. Entering that room, now abandoned once and for all, was like opening a box of memories.

Ericourt pointed to the picture and turned to Eidinger.

"Very interesting."

"Frida brought it with her from Switzerland. She frequently redecorated her room when she spent a lot of time in the same place, but she never got rid of the Scorpio picture. It was her star sign, she was born in November."

"I take it she believed in astrology."

"Absolutely. It was her religion." Eidinger took a packet of letters out of a drawer. "Here's what you asked for."

On the envelope was a name, nothing more: Gustavo.

"May I take them?" Ericourt asked. With a brief glance he had checked there were no other papers in the drawer.

"If you could read them here... There aren't many, since Frida didn't write very often. I'd rather not part with them."

He must have given them back to his wife reluctantly, now they were his again. The small victories of death.

"My secretary speaks German. He can read them."

Ericourt held the packet out to Blasi.

"Gustavo," he began to read out loud. "I feel like the happiest woman in the world to know I shall soon be there, in your country. I want to be there so much that now the mountains bear down on me like a cage. I wander through the landscape we so enjoyed together 'with eyes rendered heavy by a mournful regret for vanished illusions' like in 'Gypsies Travelling.'" Blasi stumbled over the words, and his pauses and corrections stripped the reading of any emotion. "I feel troubled by how lonely my life has become since I have been dreaming of our home in peaceful Villa Devoto, which now holds for me the same charm I once found in the Swiss lakes..."

Then the tone of the letter shifted.

"...I went to see my cousin Carlos to ask him to represent you at the ceremony. I have all the documents now. It will be funny to make my vows to him. But I am not sentimental and I can do without a traditional wedding, holding my fiancé's hand and gazing into each other's eyes as we say 'I do.'

"I shall see you soon, Gustavo. It will be so sweet to live together all that way away. 'To love at will, love and feel in the country that resembles you!' Your Frida."

The next letter had been written during the journey. Frida described how happy she was to be aboard the ship that would bring her to Buenos Aires. She shared details about the weather and very little about the passengers, since she gave the impression of being a discreet girl who talked with her fellow travellers as little as possible "to avoid their questions". She asked Gustavo to tell her about the changes he was making to the house and ended abruptly by mentioning the long hours she was spending on deck, looking over the water, her heart "distracted at times from its own clamouring by the sound of this plaint, wild and untamable".

"That's Baudelaire, from his poem 'Man and the Sea', explained Gustavo modestly. "All the quotes in the letters are from Baudelaire."

"A favourite poet of hers?"

"I imagine she had Baudelaire's poems to hand at the time. Frida was very straightforward."

Blasi was skimming through the third letter.

"She refers to some photographs here, señor Eidinger."

"Ah, yes," Eidinger said very seriously.

"Read it out," Ericourt ordered.

"I have done as you wished and brought with me the fewest possible keepsakes. You said you wanted nothing of my past, but I have not been able to part with my beloved Scorpio or some of my favourite photographs. I do not believe you will object to having at home the Frida from a while ago, before you knew me. It would be very silly to argue over that, my dear. Silly and unworthy of our reasonable love."

Gustavo was chewing the end of his unlit pipe.

"Nonsense between fiancés," he explained. "Retrospective jealously. Frida found that sort of thing amusing."

"Could you show me the photographs if you still have them?"

"Of course. They're in my studio. I wanted to enlarge them. Frida was right to bring them. They're all I have left of her now."

Once again the painful aftermath of death, the definitive abandonment made clear.

What Gustavo called his studio was up in the eaves, an attic room normally used for storage. It had been equipped to serve as a dark room. The window was boarded up with only a rhomboidal opening to let light in, which could be covered up with a specially shaped block of wood.

The photos of Frida were on the table, three in total. She wore the same stereotypical smile in all of them. In one she was wearing a swimsuit that showed off her attractive curves. The second was a portrait. The kindest comment one could make about the third was that it had surely been taken in a nudist camp. Her husband's misgivings were made sufficiently clear.

Blasi smiled to himself as he considered how the puritanical Ericourt would react. The photo had to have come from some "student body". In the background you could make out the emblem on a building. Surely the group's insignia.

The three men returned to the ground floor in silence. Muck ran down at Blasi's heels.

"He's taken a liking to you, poor thing," commented Eidinger.

An idea formed in Blasi's mind.

"If you do go away, who will you leave him with?"

Eidinger shook his head.

"There's no one I could leave him with. Frida didn't make any friends here."

Blasi bent down to pat Muck.

"In that case, leave him with me. The poor thing seems very sad."

51

"I must admit I don't know how to handle him."

"Why don't you let me take him now as a trial run? If he gets used to me then later on you can leave him with me for good."

Eidinger seemed to consider it.

"Why not? Let's give it a try," he said eventually. He went off to look for a collar and lead. Muck did not object to having them put on. Ericourt observed the scene with amusement, as if it caused no delay.

"Oh, tell me one more thing!" he exclaimed, once Eidinger had buckled the collar. "Where did you meet Czerbó?"

Eidinger straightened up and fixed his skittish eyes on Ericourt.

"Rita Czerbó came from Europe on the same boat as Frida."

"Czerbó said he knew you."

"That's true. We met through business. He must have told you that I bought material from him for my photographs. That's my hobby. I have a lot of time to spend on it. I live off my private income."

Once again, he seemed to be trying to over-explain things. Childish behaviour.

"Good day, señor Eidinger," said Ericourt as he turned to go. "We may call on you again."

He followed Blasi out. Muck was in charge of the situation. He ran happily towards the garden.

"Whatever you need," said Eidinger behind them. The door closed and the drama retreated back inside the house where memories of Frida Eidinger's life, rather than her death, lingered on. The newspapers were calling it the victim's home. Was she really the victim?

*

Ericourt was writing a private report for Blasi. As he sat at his desk, a waning moon timidly displayed its scimitar's edge through the open window.

He wrote:

  I. Do not place too much importance on coincidences. Plenty of people are interested in astrology, nudism and Baudelaire.

 II. Imagine Frida Eidinger as her letters present her, apparently reasonable but with a deep-seated fear of life that inclined her towards superstition (Scorpio), borrowing emotions she could not feel herself and with an exaggerated sense of her own worth. In other words, just the kind of person who cannot bear failure.

III. Find out if there was a failure of some kind. Her suicide would be the consequence.

 IV. Do not overlook any evidence. Muck can help us get a head start on the report we requested from the German police and find out *who* knew Frida Eidinger. That was a good idea of yours.

  V. Do not jump to conclusions. They might seem obvious but that does not mean they are correct.

 VI. Do not be too quick to assume that everyone else is mistaken.

VII. Pay private visits to any residents of the building on Calle Santa Fe you think seem interesting.

4

One Building and Many Worlds

Only a few blocks away, the trees in Plaza San Martín spread their winter branches like beautiful red-brown lacework under the hazy golden sun. It was the time of day when people are window-shopping or lazily taking a stroll. No one on Calle Santa Fe was in any hurry and they walked at a comfortable pace, enjoying the weather and not consumed by the pressing need to be anywhere.

Ferruccio Blasi had joined the flow of passers-by. Muck trotted happily at his side. The late August morning announced springtime in the clear air, the first buds and the flower stalls decorated with violets and camellias.

He crossed the threshold of the building where Andrés Torres, dressed in work clothes, was buffing the chrome door handle. Seeing them pass, Torres hurried after them with the duster in one hand and a tub of polish in the other.

"He's not a supplier," said Blasi, pointing to Muck. He knew dogs were like magnets for the ill-tempered barbs of apartment building caretakers.

He tried to slip into the service lift before the other man could begin his barrage of protests, but Torres had followed him and held the external door to stop the lift from moving.

"I have to tell you something, sir. You're from the police, aren't you?"

"We are," said Blasi, indicating his companion.

"I was actually planning on going to the police station once I'd finished the cleaning."

"Has something happened?" Blasi interrupted hopefully.

"Business of my wife's, that's all." The caretaker shook his head sullenly.

Blasi fought the desire to push him aside. He didn't have time to act as a referee for domestic disputes.

"You know what women are like, they talk and talk."

"Tell yours to keep quiet, then."

"That's even worse, she puts on such a face that I'd rather she insulted me. She says I've no right to wear trousers if I can't bring myself to talk to the police."

So something was up, after all.

"And it was right here," he pointed to the tip of his tongue, "but I couldn't manage to say it in case people thought I was afraid. My wife thinks something else is going to happen here."

Blasi burst out laughing.

"At this stage we have to call that fear rather than pre-monition."

"As you like, sir." Torres still hadn't lifted his gaze from the floor. "Ever since señor Soler came back to the building my wife has said something's going to happen. She says maybe that woman didn't commit suicide, maybe she was murdered and left in the lift as a warning to someone."

It was an original theory, at least.

"She won't leave me in peace, thinks she hears noises at night, says we don't know who's coming and going in the building and who's got keys, that we can't be downstairs watching the door twenty-four hours. She's driving me crazy."

"Pay her no notice."

"You obviously haven't heard her. Listen, sir, couldn't you send an officer to guard the door? My wife says that's what you do when there's been a crime."

"But there *hasn't* been a crime here," Blasi stressed. Tell your wife that as soon as one takes place we'll send an officer. And please let go of the door."

He pressed the button for the third floor. As the lift rose it gradually obscured the pitiful, ominous figure who was watching it go.

The Czerbós's neat apartment had the musty air of a museum. It was filled with heavy drapes, genuine rugs and second-hand furniture. Muck poked his curious nose into all the corners and his exploration of the new surroundings concluded with the owner's shoes.

Rita remained seated near a window, knitting. The curtains were almost all closed. Light was not a welcome guest in the Czerbós's home.

"Excuse me for to receive you this way," said Boris, pointing to his dressing gown. He looked taller dressed that way. His protruding cheekbones shone as brightly as his eyes under his thick, prominent eyebrows.

"We can speak German if you prefer," said Blasi in that language.

"Oh, thank you!" Boris accepted the invitation happily. "I didn't dress today. I felt tired from the interrogations these last two days. I thought they were over."

"They are over," Blasi confirmed. "I've come to see you for another reason. I'm a keen photographer and señor Eidinger told me you do enlargements."

He carefully watched the reaction to his lie. Boris Czerbó was unperturbed.

"I used to. I've since swapped my hobbies for business."

"You must miss it," Blasi said with apparent sympathy. "Photography is an art too."

"We have to live. That's another art."

Rita was listening with her chin buried in her chest. Her agile hands carried on knitting.

"Boris," she interrupted gently.

"What do you want?" When Boris spoke to his sister, all trace of the indulgent tone he used with others disappeared from his voice.

Rita said a few words in a language Blasi supposed was their mother tongue. Boris turned back to their visitor.

"My sister would like to offer you a cup of Turkish coffee."

Blasi accepted the coffee, and Rita got up to go to the kitchen. Muck, leaving his place at Blasi's feet, followed the woman.

"It seems Muck remembers your sister well."

"Who's Muck? Your dog?"

"He was señora Eidinger's dog. Don't you recognize him?"

"I never visited señora Eidinger. She never came to our house either. Her husband did."

"But your sister and señora Eidinger travelled together."

"That's true."

Something akin to a cloud was forming in the room's thick air, blurring the outlines of things, as if gas were seeping in through a crack and dulling the senses. Objectivity receded. The malign fog closed around Blasi, making him feel like he was in a different world.

He got up from his chair and went to examine a porcelain cup in the hope that a deliberate action might help him regain his lucidity.

"Dresden," he said, examining the stamp on the cup.

"Yes."

"On the subject of stamps," said Blasi distractedly, "I wonder if you could help me decipher one I saw yesterday in a photograph."

Boris's sunken eyes shone with irony.

"Is that a personal or a professional request?"

"Think of it as both."

Boris leant back in an armchair and, looking towards the kitchen door, called out:

"Rita!"

She appeared in no more than a couple of seconds. Her brother gestured to the cigarette holder that lay on a side table. Rita muttered a few words in Bulgarian. Muck stuck his rectangular head around the door. Boris spoke to Blasi again.

"Please excuse the scene." Feeling herself ignored once more, Rita disappeared through the inner door. "My sister forgets all sorts of things. The war affected her deeply. One has to explain her duties to her as to a small child. Fortunately there are two cigarettes left in the case and I'm able to offer you one."

Blasi could have quite happily hurled the silver cigarette case at his head. He hadn't been wrong to judge Boris as a hateful human being who liked to lord it over others whenever he got the chance.

Rita appeared with a tray and poured the coffee. She then went back to her knitting by the window. While the men drank their coffee she played with Muck. She threw the ball of wool for him and the little dog ran to bring it back to her lap.

The game did nothing to dispel the pallor of her cheeks or her worried expression. She threw the ball of wool and picked it up distractedly. She was a woman absent from her movements.

"It seems Muck and your sister get on very well," said Blasi.

"For the moment. Rita is unstable and incapable of focusing on one thing for long."

Rita accepted the comment with her usual passivity.

"I must go," said Blasi, standing up. "I'm sorry we haven't been able to make an arrangement."

"It was one possible outcome." Czerbó had also stood up and was the first to hold out his hand. "I'm sorry too."

"Come on, Muck!"

The fox terrier, hearing his name, ran towards Blasi. Rita stared at him with vacant eyes. She automatically followed Blasi after he had already said goodbye to Boris, who apologized for not seeing him to the door. She brought with her all the listlessness that stripped the Czerbós's home of any human warmth. Her fear was palpable. Blasi could finally name the mephitic gas that anaesthetized one's will upon entering the apartment. A fear that weighed as heavily as a tombstone on a world of tiny wriggling larvae, smothering them without squashing or immobilizing them.

Blasi deliberately stretched out his departure, slowly taking his overcoat and hat from the stand. Rita waited motionlessly.

"Say goodbye to Muck, señorita Czerbó," said Blasi, patting her shoulder as if wanting to show his approval. Without saying a word, she turned and walked back into the apartment.

Aurora Torres was right, there was a bad omen floating around that house. Lost in his thoughts, Blasi did not notice the lift stopping on the second floor. The door opened to let

Betty in. On recognizing Blasi she could not contain a grimace of annoyance. The young man gave her an involuntarily unctuous smile.

"Today's your lucky day," he said in reply to her greeting.

"Don't try to copyright that as a conversation starter. I've heard it a thousand times."

"I'm not saying that because we met but because I was just thinking of going to see you. As you're on your way out, how about we walk a few blocks together?"

Betty agreed with a silent shrug of her shoulders. They had reached the ground floor.

"Is this your dog?" Muck had launched himself at Betty's low-heeled shoes, stopping her from moving. "He seems intelligent."

"If you mean that by way of contrast, thank you for the general idea you've formed of me."

"Someone once told me that thinking too quickly is the same as a bad round of golf. The ball never goes far."

Blasi observed her smilingly.

"I've heard plenty about you, but no one mentioned your irresistible fondness for aphorism. How is señor Iñarra?"

"Fine, thank you. He had a relapse yesterday but Dr Luchter recommended some electric treatments that have helped. All this makes things terribly difficult for poor Gaby."

Blasi's reproachful look did not go unnoticed.

"Don't think me insensitive. Let me explain why. It all comes from my father's overprotectiveness. He had the machine installed by someone on his list of protégés—the laundry delivery boy, can you imagine! As a result we're left in the dark half the time."

Ferruccio burst out laughing.

"It does me good to talk to you. I feel like I've escaped a snake pit."

Betty did not respond.

"He's a nice dog," she said, pointing at Muck. "Have you had him long?"

"No, he's been entrusted to me so I can carry out some very instructive exercises."

All around them were the luxurious shopfronts of Calle Santa Fe. They had joined the carefree milieu and, like the others in the street, they maintained an impersonal tone of conversation. Betty said hello to a few people as they passed.

"You're obviously rather popular," Ferruccio joked.

"That's exactly what the caretaker's wife says. And she won't let it go. She loves martyrs. I'm sure she thinks I'm too happy."

"Other people always end up seeing us as martyrs to something or someone," was Blasi's verdict.

Betty's dismissively upturned nose did not herald a friendly response.

"Now I know why you said that about my fondness for aphorism. It seems you're easily infected."

Blasi let the jibe go unacknowledged and they walked a little way in silence. Suddenly, Betty came at him with a direct question.

"How's the investigation going?"

"It's been closed."

"Oh, yes? What were you doing at the Czerbós's apartment, then?"

"A private matter," replied Blasi, pointing at Muck.

Betty seemed sceptical.

"Shall we have a drink in that bar?" she suggested. "I want to ask you something and I need a stiff drink first."

They looked for a secluded table. Blasi ordered two double whiskies and Betty did not object. While he spoke to the waiter, she slowly removed her gloves and laid them on her purse with the good manners proper to the daughter of the upright señor Iñarra.

"That'll give you plenty of courage," Blasi said, laughing. "But if it's a matter of the heart, spare me because I'll find it hard to hear."

"Sort of… Do you promise you'll be frank with me?"

"Listen, that wasn't the deal. You were going to ask me something."

"I'm getting to that. Will I be questioned again?"

Their drinks had been served, and Betty lifted the glass to her lips, apparently concentrating on the task of drinking the whisky without disturbing the ice cubes at the bottom.

"I can't promise you won't, but it's unlikely."

After taking a couple of sips, Betty placed her glass on the table and cupped it in both hands.

"What did Rita say to you?" she asked.

Her eyes had lost their sardonic shine and were fixed on Blasi with trusting warmth.

"Why do you suppose she said something to me?"

"It doesn't matter. I'm going to tell you anyway," Betty sighed. "I need some advice and you seem like the best person to ask."

She stretched out her hand towards him.

"I want you to understand. What I'm going to tell you isn't anything bad, but I couldn't say it… It would make things unnecessarily complicated at home. The night of señora Eidinger's death, I was with Boris Czerbó."

An uncomfortable weight plummeted in Blasi's stomach. To encourage Betty he returned the half-smile she offered as bait.

"I got home from the cinema before one a.m.," she went on, "and I went straight to the Czerbós's apartment. I often did that when I went out at night. Boris was waiting for me. My visits weren't what you're thinking; we used to meet at that time to avoid comments from Rita, who isn't as harmless as she seems. She's jealous of her brother's friendships and I wanted to avoid any trouble."

"What trouble would there have been if your relationship with Czerbó is as innocent as you make out?"

"It's because of my father. He doesn't trust anyone. He would have been against it. Sometimes I think that the fact I'm trusting and like making friends is a reaction against him. Ever since I was little he's terrified me with his distrust. And, even so, you see what I'm capable of. It's not like me to be telling a secret to a police officer."

The uncomfortable, oppressive feeling in Blasi's stomach seemed to double.

"Are you trying to tell me that your visits to Czerbó are the result of a childish desire to rebel?" he asked sarcastically.

Betty was staring into her glass again.

"If you interrogate me like that you'll make me regret telling you. I just wanted you to tell me if I should keep quiet about my visit that night. I'd prefer to, of course, but my confession could constitute a defence for Boris Czerbó."

"No one's accusing him, so you can keep quiet. Did anyone see you leave the apartment?"

The question was obviously unexpected because Betty didn't hide her surprise.

"I don't know. I hadn't thought about it. I'd just got in when Torres came to get us. Gabriela might have heard me. She spends a lot of nights awake. Dad's illness has destroyed her nerves."

"She ought to get some fresh air. Doesn't she ever go out?"

"Hardly ever. She's got such an exaggerated sense of responsibility that you could load all the world's problems onto her and she'd be convinced it was her job to sort them out."

"Do you blame your father for that, too?" Blasi asked with friendly sarcasm.

"I don't blame anyone. I say things as I see them."

Two or three tugs of the lead let Blasi know that Muck wanted a change of scene. It annoyed him to have to comply. Any interruption of his conversation with Betty could mean a change of tack that might not favour him, but he feared a disaster if he did not obey the pressing appeals reaching him via the leather lead.

"Would you excuse us?" he said, gesturing to Muck. "Paternal responsibilities. Order another round while I'm gone."

As he waited outside with forced acquiescence, he asked himself why Betty had decided to make such a confession to him. Their meeting in the lift had been unexpected, which meant her confidences were not premeditated. Was she suspicious of Czerbó? Was she afraid that he had talked first? What was the point of associating herself with such an unpleasant man as the Bulgarian ex-photographer? The answer to any of these questions could represent a change in the orbit of the moon that Ericourt had mentioned.

From the door he saw Betty hunched over, brooding. Away from the public gaze she was a simple girl with a genuine, honest expression. As he walked back to the table to join her, he noticed she was staring over his shoulder with a look of surprise. Hadn't she expected to carry on with the conversation?

"There's no mistaking you," said Dr Luchter behind him. "I spotted you from the corner when you were coming into the bar and it occurred to me that Betty would be with you."

So that was why.

"Have a seat, Doctor. We've just ordered a second round."

"Why were you looking for me, Doctor?" Betty couldn't hide her discomfort.

"Don't worry, Betty," Luchter answered distractedly as he tried to get the waiter's attention. "I've just paid a quick visit to your father at señora de Iñarra's request. I gave him an injection."

"But Dad was fine when I left the house."

"It was a simple precaution. Your mother was alarmed for no reason."

Betty picked up her purse and gloves.

"I'd better be going, then. If Dad hasn't been feeling well this morning I don't want to give him any reason to complain by making lunch late. Thank you for the drink, señor Blasi. I'll leave you with Dr Luchter."

It was not a bad game of hide-and-seek. Blasi lifted his glass once more, inviting his companion to join him in a toast.

"To the happy conclusion of the inquiries. I imagine they've been rather a nuisance for you."

He peered sidelong at Muck, who was sniffing the doctor's shoes.

"It's not a problem. I've learned not to concern myself with other people's business."

"I envy you that ability. Give me the recipe for when I'm sitting in the cinema next to one of those women who can't help but comment on the film."

Luchter was working his way through the peanuts, shelling them with the tips of his fingers before dropping them into his mouth from above. It was time for a change of subject.

"I'd like to ask you a question," said Blasi, feigning seriousness now. "Do you think it can ever work to give up everything that reminds one of a difficult time in life?"

"We doctors are not fond of abstractions," replied Luchter, unflappable. "If you're referring to a particular case I'd rather discuss it as such. We deal with patients, not diseases."

"I was thinking of Czerbó."

"I'm not particularly familiar with his case."

"It's an interesting one. You must've met plenty of men like him. People who take up a new profession because they need to completely forget the past."

"If I've met people like that the best I can do is put a considerable distance between them and myself. They were the reason I left my country."

"Do you mean to say you left voluntarily?"

Luchter was still methodically eating the peanuts. Muck was dozing at Blasi's feet with his head on his front paws. Blasi shot him an envious look.

Ten minutes more of conversation with this lump of lead and I'll be doing the same, chum, he thought.

"You're a good assistant," he heard Luchter say.

"On the contrary. My boss says I take too much initiative."

"In any case I'm going to tell you what you shouldn't ask me so as not to reoffend on that count. I stated yesterday that I wasn't ever part of any political associations, student bodies or nudist colonies in my country."

"How can you have kept yourself to yourself to that degree?"

"Because I've only ever been interested in my career. Do you want my whole life story?"

"I know it, thank you. Adolfo Federico Luchter, son of a

Lutheran pastor, Juan Federico Luchter, and Margarita Oederle, who died in 1928. Born in Munich on the 28th of September 1910. Only child. Your father was arrested by a paramilitary group in 1939. Disappeared. Presumed dead. You studied medicine in Munich and left Germany in 1935. You lived for three years in Paris. Is there anything else? Oh, yes! There is no known link between you and Frida Eidinger."

"Absolutely," declared Dr Luchter. "And now will you allow me to call the waiter?"

"Absolutely," said Blasi approvingly.

5

The Web

vii. Pay private visits to any residents of the building on Calle Santa Fe you think seem interesting.

Blasi had been feeling torn since Betty had confided in him. His sense of professionalism was at odds with his personal feelings, and over the next three days something stopped him acting on the last point of Santiago Ericourt's recommendations any time he found a sliver of time in his work that would have allowed it.

It was no good telling himself he should talk to Betty again even if the issue of her visits to the Czerbós had nothing to do with the circumstances of Frida Eidinger's death. He was always so busy! Inspector Ericourt was forever mentioning more people who were in some way linked to the dead woman. He had to find them, listen to them, hear new names, track down others. And in the background of all that coming and going was the uncomfortable twinge of the secret.

Since Betty was with Czerbó at the time of señora Eidinger's death, neither could be involved in the matter and as such it was no use mentioning a relationship that had nothing to do with the investigation. The point was not to discover what intimacy existed between the two of them, but rather any Frida Eidinger might have shared with someone else.

He told himself this for the hundredth time as he was preparing to enter his boss's office that morning. Santiago Ericourt received him looking his best. His lively gaze, rosy face and the agility of his movements all indicated a man ready to spring into action.

"News," he said, pointing happily to the telephone. "A call from Eidinger. He wants to talk to me. We're going over there."

"Has something happened?"

Why did he feel as if he had just been punched in the stomach? He really was on edge.

"It seems so. I knew someone would end up feeling the need to talk."

Until that moment Inspector Ericourt's official conclusion had been that the case was a suicide planned to trouble the supposed guilty party. "Generally," he liked to say, "when women in love kill themselves it's to get revenge on someone equally weak who has been unable to manage the situation."

As they climbed into the police car, Blasi, who knew the intensity of Ericourt's self-absorption, suggested humbly:

"Shall I drive?"

"No, let me. I feel very lively this morning."

"Lord help us," sighed Blasi.

They set off with Ericourt at the wheel. All of a sudden the Inspector said, in a voice so distant it proved to Blasi the danger they were in:

"The man over whom Frida Eidinger committed suicide is keeping quiet out of fear. Deep down it's a matter of no consequence, a simple personal problem."

"Crimes tend to be personal problems," said Blasi, who felt inclined towards pessimism that morning.

"It's not a crime. If someone killed her there would've been better ways to get rid of the key ring."

"There can be cases of mental confusion, can't there? Anyway, the keys were found by chance."

"You're right," admitted Ericourt.

He must have set off along a new path of conjectures. Blasi saw the back of a red truck fill the car's windscreen, almost flat against the bonnet.

"Watch out!" he shouted.

"I've interrogated more than twenty people," went on Ericourt calmly. "No one knows anything. You've heard the neighbours and friends. They all say it seemed like a perfect marriage. Frida didn't have a social life, she was a good housewife, she didn't shirk her duties."

"Reserved, haughty and spurning friendships, according to local gossip. You call that a good image?"

"More than one husband would think it ideal."

"I'm single. Any theory about the perfect woman—"

He didn't finish formulating his thought. The driver of a bus passing too close flung a few choice phrases at him as he went by, making several references to family members, along with a gesture that made their meaning perfectly clear. Blasi opted for silence.

They took a side street where Ericourt could give himself over to speculation without further incidents. A few minutes later they arrived at the house on Calle Lácar.

Eidinger hadn't lost his resemblance to a rat sniffing around a cave. He took a few minutes to come to the door.

"Forgive me, I was upstairs," he explained as he beckoned them in. "I keep wandering around doing nothing. I can't get used to being alone."

It was true, the place had become the charmless refuge of a desolate man. It was as if Frida's presence had disappeared

70

completely. The unpleasant grey day filtered into the house. Blasi examined the small living room, looking for material evidence of the change. He noted the absence of Frida's photograph. Eidinger watched his movements warily.

"How's Muck?" he asked.

"Very well."

"You can bring him back tomorrow. I'll keep him until I decide to go away. I've started to miss the bother he caused me. I felt better with him here."

The endearing melancholy of a simple man, but had he called just to tell them he missed Muck?

"What happened?" Ericourt tackled the issue head-on.

Eidinger sat in front of him, his eyes downcast.

"Last night I got a strange, threatening phone call. They said I should immediately destroy the photographs of Frida if I didn't want anything to happen to me."

"What time was that?"

"Midnight."

"Did you recognize the voice?"

"It was a man's voice. He sounded threatening and spoke perfect Spanish. The voice didn't seem disguised."

Ericourt listened behind a mask of seriousness, with his eyes half-closed.

"And did you destroy the photographs?"

The fact that he had called them made it seem unlikely that he had. However, more than nine hours had passed since the mysterious call. Fear doesn't wait that long to raise the alarm.

"They're in my studio as usual."

"You should've called straight away."

71

"Why? It was ridiculous. Nothing could happen. Both doors are locked. And the windows have bars. No one could get in."

"You might've had an unexpected visit."

"I wouldn't have let any stranger in."

"It needn't necessarily be a stranger."

Eidinger looked at the Inspector, seemingly wounded.

"I've spent the night thinking, Inspector. Do you remember Frida's letters? She insisted on bringing those photos with her even though she knew I didn't want her to. She refused to destroy them or get rid of them, which made me think they meant a lot to her. After her death I felt sorry I'd been so pig-headed. Now I think my wife was hiding something from me, and not necessarily a matter of the heart."

Ericourt's face had darkened.

"Bring me those photographs right away. Blasi will go up and stay with you until we send an officer. You won't be left by yourself in this house or go out alone until this matter has been resolved."

Eidinger walked towards the stairs looking perplexed. Blasi followed him. Just as they crossed the hall, a woman's scream came from above, a sharp screech of fear that rooted them both to the spot.

Eidinger was the first to come to his senses and run up the stairs. Blasi hurled himself after him. All of a sudden he felt Ericourt violently push past, breathing heavily.

On the first floor landing they heard a muffled whine.

"Carry on… it's further up…" panted Ericourt.

Blasi bounded up to the attic landing. There he met Eidinger, who was rubbing his forehead. At his feet was a tray, the kind used for developing photographs. The screams had stopped.

Blasi took out his lighter and used it to illuminate the space behind the half-open door. A single glance was enough to reveal the female form pressed against the back wall. He heard Ericourt's voice behind him once more.

"Come out with your hands up," he ordered. He had taken out his revolver.

Betty Iñarra appeared in the doorway. Blasi looked at her in astonishment, holding the lighter in his hand like a tiny torch of truth. The flame singed his fingers and he put it out, cursing.

"Who else is in there?" asked Ericourt.

"No one," said Betty firmly.

"What were you doing there?"

"Tell them," implored Eidinger. "There's no point hiding it now."

"Be quiet," thundered Ericourt. "I'm the one talking. What were you doing in there and why did you scream?"

"There was someone else in there," stammered Betty. "I thought he was going to attack me but he escaped..."

"That's impossible," protested Eidinger.

"What were you doing in there?" asked Ericourt for the third time.

"I was hiding. I came to see señor Eidinger and we were on the first floor when you arrived. I told him it wouldn't do for you to find me here. He asked me to wait up here until you'd gone. When he went downstairs I looked for a safer place to hide and found this attic room. I opened the door and went in..."

Betty ran her gaze, which seemed a plea for help, over the three expectant men.

"I couldn't see anything. The only light was a slit from that opening in the window. All of a sudden I sensed I wasn't alone.

I felt my heart stop and I tried to calm down and convince myself it was only fear, but just then the slit of light divided in two. I couldn't help screaming, then the door opened and a man ran out. I was in the dark again. I stretched out my hand and grabbed something. The door creaked and I threw what I was holding with all my strength at whoever was coming in. I didn't realize it was señor Eidinger. I'm so sorry."

It was funny to apologize for having attacked someone and almost split his head open in such circumstances. Her good education took over at that moment, making her forget the aggressive self-confidence she usually adopted around others.

"Is that true?" said Ericourt to Eidinger.

"Yes, it's true."

"What was she doing in your house?"

Betty and Eidinger exchanged a brief glance.

"Tell him," he pleaded.

"I came to see a picture I was interested in buying."

She looked like a shaggy dog that had accidentally fallen into a bathtub of water.

"It can't be true," Eidinger insisted. "If someone was in there they can't have got out of the house. The back door is secured with a padlock and no one could have gone out the front without passing us."

"Search the attic," Ericourt ordered Blasi. "Bring the photographs."

Blasi went into the attic room. The window was closed as usual. Eidinger had followed him. He heard an exclamation of surprise and turned. Gustavo was looking in horror at the workbench.

"They really have taken them," he murmured. "Run, do something."

"What? I don't suppose I'll find the suspect on the street corner."

Ericourt's head appeared round the door.

"Come out of there," he said. "We'll search the attic later. Lock the door and give me the key."

They walked downstairs with Ericourt bringing up the rear, clutching his revolver. When they were in the hall he ordered Blasi to conduct a full search of the house, taking Eidinger with him.

"And call the station. Have them send the fingerprint team and a female police auxiliary. You come with me," he said to Betty, directing her into the living room.

She faced him with serene courage, like a soldier resigned to battle.

"What was the picture you mentioned? How did you know about it?"

"Señor Czerbó told me about a picture of señora Eidinger's, an engraving of the symbol for Scorpio. I came to see it this morning."

"And señor Eidinger received you without any objection. Did he know who you were?"

"I called yesterday afternoon to tell him I'd be coming."

"What did you do with the photographs? You came here looking for them."

Betty frowned.

"I don't understand what you mean."

"You and your accomplice had a plan. Eidinger would be sure to call the police after you threatened him. Your visit would coincide with ours. You let your accomplice in and helped him escape, didn't you?"

Betty pursed her lips.

"No, that isn't true. No."

"Was it Czerbó?"

"No."

Ericourt walked over to the window and lifted the blind to look out into the street. He drummed his fingers on the glass.

"In a moment," he announced, turning suddenly, "our people will be here. If you have the photographs with you we'll find them. If you've hidden them somewhere in the house we'll also find them. You'd better tell the truth."

"I have told the truth," Betty replied curtly.

Blasi, who was at the living room door again having concluded his search with Eidinger, caught these last words and looked at Betty with distrust and resentment.

"The back door was padlocked," he said. "I've called the station. They're on their way."

"Fine, in the meantime check the garden to see if there are any footprints. They might've thrown the photographs out the window."

Betty smiled ironically.

"Why did the young lady call you yesterday?" the Inspector asked Gustavo.

"To ask if she could visit. She was interested in the Scorpio picture, she said. I asked her to come at this time. I've been thinking about it: why would she warn me if she was coming to my house to steal the photographs?"

"Leave the hypothesizing to me. That's my job," Ericourt reminded him.

With his eyes fixed on the floor, Eidinger looked the sorry picture of a man who deep down is in turmoil.

"I'd better explain myself. I understand that it was a mistake not to do so sooner, but try to understand me. Frida was my wife."

An impatient gesture from Ericourt told him he would do well to skip any unnecessary detail.

"What I mean is, I've tried to talk as little as possible to stop any publicity about things I wasn't sure of. Frida's guardedness and reticence had made me suspicious of late. I guessed she had a secret and I decided to watch her behaviour and her movements. Frida was keen to track down certain people who had emigrated from Germany, and I know it's stupid but I was overcome with jealousy every time I saw her worry about one of them. All the same, events proved me wrong and I always ended up convinced of her fidelity."

He paused.

"Carry on, Eidinger." The Inspector's voice was authoritative.

"I don't know how or why it occurred to me afterwards to think she might have different motives to the ones I'd suspected up to then. Do you see? I was tortured by mistrust. It weighed on my conscience. I spent my days imagining scenarios and came to the conclusion that Frida's apparently innocent curiosity was covering up a plan."

"Amateur detectives," Ericourt muttered through his teeth.

"Frida only brought her personal documents and those blasted photographs with her. She was vain, her desire to keep them seemed very straightforward."

"Did you employ a professional to follow your wife?"

Eidinger shook his head.

"Why not? That would have been the most sensible."

"They're expensive," Eidinger admitted humbly. "I couldn't afford it."

But Frida was a rich woman. Had she been tight-fisted with her husband? Was that the cause of their marital disagreements? Or had Eidinger felt it morally wrong to use his wife's money as a weapon against her?

"You will recall," Eidinger went on, "that in one of the photographs there was a door behind Frida bearing some insignia. She told me it belonged to a student body. I thought that perhaps if I knew more about that organization it would guide the thread of my investigation. I knew the photograph had been taken in Hamburg near a summer camp."

"My God! All those investigations would be very expensive, too."

"I have friends in Germany. I spoke with Czerbó and asked him to help me make an enlargement of the emblem. He was noncommittal."

"What did he say exactly?"

"That he'd left the business. It was the day before Frida's death. I was readier than ever to do the job. And now…"

"Why didn't you tell us about all this before, señor Eidinger? Didn't it occur to you that this might be of interest to the police?"

Eidinger was not in control of his nerves. He frowned and rubbed his hands against his thighs.

"I know I was wrong, but you have to understand, I couldn't accuse Frida without being sure."

This struck Ericourt as foolish, and foolish motivations invariably end up complicit in the criminal actions of others.

The doorbell rang. A car had stopped outside the house. A van was about to do the same. The "backup" had arrived. Ericourt went to let them in, leaving Betty with the female police auxiliary tasked with searching her clothing. The girl behaved herself. She seemed not to even blink.

A current of healthy activity began to flow around the house. Ericourt told Blasi to call Czerbó and say he would be stopping by. The fingerprinting team were beginning their nosy search of the past. The automatic thinking of the men whose job it was to construct an event outside its real place in time unleashed a chain of possibilities: climbing of walls, forced locks, fingerprints, footprints. Clues blossomed on powdered surfaces. The photographer ran back and forth.

The female police auxiliary planted herself in front of Ericourt:

"I haven't found anything in the suspect's clothing, sir. Should I take care of the transfer?"

The two women, Betty with her haughty reserve and the irritable, overbearing auxiliary, found each other intolerable. Betty waited behind the other woman, her pallor draining all the charm from her features.

"I'll accompany the young lady," said Ericourt.

Where had Blasi got to? He'd been keen to get out of there. Routine practices bored him terribly. Oh, yes! He would be calling the Czerbós's apartment.

Blasi rushed down the stairs.

"Caramba, look where you're going!" screeched one of the photographers.

Blasi's agitation was disguised among the bustle of newcomers.

"Sir," he said in a low voice when he was next to Ericourt. "I've just called. They found Czerbó dead in his room. There are officers already there."

6

The Horsefly

Boris Czerbó's body was lying in his bed. The curtains had been drawn back and the light of a cottony midday merged with the yellowish skin stretched over his prominent cheekbones. Brachycephalic skull, observed Ericourt privately, surrendering to an untimely thought that served to release some pressure in his overburdened mind. Purplish marks were appearing around Czerbó's eyes and the slow draining of colour gradually highlighted the imperfections of his face. On his left cheek was the pale button of a wart.

Lahore was also next to the bed.

"We received the call approximately an hour ago. His sister found him. She said she hadn't woken him early because Dr Luchter advised her to let him sleep. Last night he came to see him."

"Who rang the station? Did she?"

"No, Soler did. Señorita Czerbó ran to get help. Do you want to question anyone straight away?"

"Not yet."

On a side table there was an ashtray with a cigarette stub, a used match and a strip of paper that was singed at one end. Next to the ashtray, the kind of cardboard box commonly used by pharmacies as a container for capsules and two glasses; in one of them discoloured prunes floated in brownish, cloudy water. The other was empty.

"What does it say?" said Ericourt, pointing to the paper.

"It looks like a rendezvous. Some words have been burnt. I can only read 'you tonight'. It's typewritten."

"And what did the medical report say?"

"He died ten or twelve hours ago. Cyanide, just like the other case. I'm going to send the ashtray and everything else to the laboratory at once. Where were you? I sent for you."

"Following the trail of some souvenir hunters. I've just witnessed the Argentinian version of *The Mystery of the Yellow Room* with a fifty-year-old Rouletabille weighing eighty-five kilos. That's me."

He covered Czerbó's face with a sheet. Death had not disfigured him in its merciful prolongation of sleep.

They went into the adjoining room, the dead man's study. Lahore drummed his fingers on the scratched leather of the desk as he listened to Ericourt's account. The midday sun stripped the second-hand furniture of the mask of decency usually provided by the gloom in the Czerbós's home.

"So far they've found no trace of the photographs or the thief. We'll see if they come across any suspicious fingerprints."

"What do you think?"

"I'm a rationalist. I've never been tempted by three-legged tables."

"The girl lied."

"That's the most likely. She had time to tear up the photographs and throw them down the toilet. Is Vera here? Send him to get señorita Iñarra, have him take her to the station. And tell Blasi to come here. He's at Eidinger's house. We'll need him to interpret when we question Czerbó's sister."

Lahore went to call Blasi. In the living room he found Soler,

Andrés and two officers. The caretaker's expression, which seemed to say "I told you so", puzzled the Superintendent.

When he returned to the desk he found Ericourt smoking with distasteful enjoyment.

"Do you believe it was suicide?" asked Lahore.

"Yes, two suicides in the same building and a girl who's a compulsive liar. Some coincidence."

Lahore squirmed gently in his seat, like a cat that feels someone is tying a dog to its tail.

"I don't believe one word of that story about the photographs."

"There could be someone else involved. Strangers who were threatening Frida and Czerbó. Maybe Czerbó sent Iñarra's daughter to get hold of a compromising piece of evidence."

"Why her, when she didn't know him?"

"We can't be sure of that. Rita will tell us *who* was in the apartment yesterday."

"Luchter was there. I've sent for him. They didn't find him at home or at the hospital."

"He must be out on visits."

"I don't like this business."

"There's no need to be nervous. I'm just getting to like it."

An officer asked to have a word with the Superintendent. Lahore called him in.

"You'd better hear this man out, Superintendent, sir. He says he's not going anywhere until he's spoken to you."

"Who is it?"

"The caretaker."

"Send him in," advised Ericourt. "He'll have nothing to say, mark my words. They never talk when they should."

Andrés Torres appeared. There was a prologue that included the inevitable refrains, "women's stuff" and "mine never leaves me in peace", while he repeatedly ran his hand over the back of his shaved head, his eyes glued to the floor.

But he did have something to say, after all. Soler and Czerbó had had an argument, months ago, in Soler's apartment. His wife was there because she had been covering for Soler's maid, who was unwell. The two men had shut themselves in the study because Czerbó insisted on "talking alone". Soon after, Aurora heard raised voices and then saw Soler shoving the other man out. After the door had closed, she heard him say that one day "he was going to give himself the pleasure of squashing him like a cockroach."

"What was the argument about?"

"My wife says they were talking about a woman, and this morning señor Soler came to see me and warned me not to tell anyone about the episode. He said it was silly but he didn't want any trouble."

"You clearly took his advice," said Ericourt mockingly.

"I thought, señor Inspector, that I ought to help the police. It's our duty."

"And you've done yours. You can calm down now."

He imagined Czerbó's motionless body as he had seen it a few moments earlier. An unfortunate soul who only ever attracted bad feeling. He had slipped like a reptile into the others' lives. A blackmailer, Ericourt said to himself—I guessed as much.

Rita entered the room. The life had drained from her pinched and faded features, not even fear remained. She dragged her feet as she walked and her arms hung limply at her sides. Blasi remembered how she had followed him into the hall the day of his visit with Muck. Then, even her listless obedience and her slavish automatism had indicated some spirit. Now it was worse. Rita Czerbó has become a ghost, a shadow outliving its body.

All the same, she responded to the questions with extraordinary fluency and precision. She stated that the previous day her brother had seemed nervous and irritable. These crises, which were followed by sleepless nights and bouts of deep nervous depression, were familiar. At Boris's request she had called Dr Luchter. The doctor had come at eight p.m. He prescribed some tranquillizing capsules and personally took the prescription to the pharmacy to have them prepared. He came back with them at ten p.m. and advised Rita to go and get some rest, saying he would stay with Boris until the medicine took effect. He warned her that Boris would probably sleep for a long time, so she should not worry if he stayed in bed later than usual.

Rita did as she was told and went to her room. She always locked the door and that night she did so trusting that her brother would not need her again. She did not hear Dr Luchter leave the apartment because her bedroom was at the end of the hall, separated from Boris's by an anteroom, the study and his bathroom.

That was all. She got up early. She served Boris's breakfast. She was not surprised that he had not called for it. She did the cleaning and then went out to run an errand.

"Where did you go?"

"To the laundry. The previous day I'd had an incident with Boris…"

Boris had been very nervous lately and told her not to let any strangers in. The previous morning the young man from the laundry had called by. It was not their day but he explained that a ticket had been lost which he assumed she had not given back. He asked her to look carefully for it to avoid any trouble with his employers. She looked for the ticket to no avail. When she returned to the kitchen (the lad had called at the service entrance, of course) there was no one there.

"I didn't think anything of it," Rita went on, "but I told Boris all the same. He called the laundry and they told him the lad hadn't turned up that afternoon. They had the ticket. Boris blamed me, saying I would be responsible for whatever happened."

Always the same droning voice, stripped of any nuance of tone, innocuous as a stream of distilled water, echoless as a punch thrown at a feather cushion.

"The young man still hadn't turned up this morning. I went home. It was time to make lunch. I thought I should tell Boris. I always told him everything. That was when I found him."

The slow, monotonous wave stopped. Rita was still staring at the interior window. On the opposite side there was a greyish wall with long teary streaks of soot and rain.

"Get the number for the laundry and find that young man," Lahore ordered Blasi.

The questioning started up again. Blasi mentally classified the missing information as something that would have to wait to be resolved because he was busy with the task at hand.

"Did anyone ever visit your brother at night?" asked Lahore.

Blasi repeated the question in German.

"Oh, yes!"

Almost at the same time as he heard the answer, Blasi had to formulate the next question. A clerk was writing constantly.

"Who?"

"A woman."

"How do you know?"

Rita pointed to the door leading to the hall.

"You spied on them?"

She nodded.

"Did you know who the woman was?"

Blasi was trying hard to remain professional.

"Señorita Iñarra," he translated unnecessarily. The name had been perfectly clear.

"Tell señorita Czerbó she's free to go."

Rita muttered a few words in a language Blasi did not understand.

"What's she saying now?"

"I don't know. She's not speaking German."

"Ask her."

The angry drumming of Lahore's fingers accompanied Rita's explanation.

"She's afraid to be left alone."

"An officer will go with her. Get her out of here. Bring señorita Iñarra in. You, go and do what I asked."

Blasi hesitated. Which was worse, silence or an ill-timed explanation? He decided to keep quiet. Betty passed him in the hall while he was instructing one of the officers to stay with Rita.

"She'll say no more than she wants to," he thought. He now knew it was the young woman's strong will bubbling below the surface that made her eyes shine.

Ericourt also identified in her gaze the energy of an instinct for self-preservation that gradually pushes the soul to its last defences. It was he who began the interrogation.

"Señorita Iñarra, señorita Czerbó has told us you'd been visiting her brother late at night, is that true?"

"Yes," said Betty, very sure of herself.

"When did these visits start?"

"About a month ago."

"Did you come here every night?"

"No, only occasionally."

How could one explain her apparent repulsion at hearing such a simple question?

"Did señorita Czerbó know about your visits?"

"I didn't think she did, until now."

"So you kept your visits a secret."

"Yes."

"Why?"

Betty bit her bottom lip.

"For the same reason such visits are usually kept secret," she said with the air of superiority adopted by those who aim to strip all importance from something they know will be viewed badly. "My family didn't think highly of Czerbó."

"And was that how you learned from señor Czerbó about señora Eidinger's engraving?"

"Yes."

"That is to say you saw señor Czerbó after the 23rd of August."

"I only saw him once."

"Did you arrange to meet him yesterday?"

With a look the girl measured up the two men who were scrutinizing her words and gestures.

"A rendezvous typed on a slip of paper... Yes, that was me. I told him I wanted to see him last night. I sent him the note in a pack of cigarettes Rita came to get for him. I thought it was a good way to tell Boris I wanted to talk to him."

"When did you write it?"

"In the afternoon."

"Did you always arrange to meet that way?"

"Sometimes, when we couldn't use the telephone. Because of my father," she clarified.

"Why didn't you send the note as soon as you'd written it?"

"I was waiting for an opportunity to send it to him. Rita often came to us for help to get out of scrapes. She's very forgetful. I didn't absolutely need to see Boris that night, after all. If I didn't get a chance to announce my visit I could leave it for another time."

"And did you come here that night?"

"No, I waited for a phone call from Boris answering my note… He didn't call."

Ericourt paused and offered Betty a cigarette.

"I don't smoke," replied the girl.

The Inspector exchanged a glance with Lahore.

"Why did you go to señor Eidinger's house?" Ericourt attacked.

"I told you. I wanted to see the picture."

Someone called from the laboratory to speak to Superintendent Lahore. Ericourt and the young woman were left alone.

"You didn't time your request very well," said the Inspector, taking up his questioning again.

"I didn't think that. I thought it was most natural."

Would she be so cynical as to feign naivety? After what she had just revealed about her relationship with Czerbó her position seemed hardly credible.

"How did you justify the request?"

"I didn't. I simply told him the reason for my visit."

Horizontal furrows lined Betty's forehead, and a red patch was spreading across it. She had taken off her green silk scarf and the same patch was continuing down her neck. She was lying, then. Who was she trying to protect? Herself? Someone else?

"If I'm arrested," she said suddenly in a faltering voice, "I'd like you to be the one to tell my father."

Ericourt sat up straight in his seat. The appeal to his leniency made him angry, as if she had identified a weakness in him.

"What did you do with the photographs?" he thundered.

"I don't have them," Betty stammered. "I don't know anything about them."

She broke off. Lahore rushed into the room like a man leading a troop.

"They found cyanide in one of the capsules," he said all at once. His thoughts seemed to have travelled a long way in a short amount of time. "I've already notified the Examining Magistrate."

Soler was sitting opposite Luchter, waiting for the Examining Magistrate to call him in to make a statement. It was all highly unusual, and consequently ridiculous. When one has lived among other people who have, directly or indirectly, known one since one was a chubby ball in nappies already participating in family life, one cannot run the risk of having them think one is involved in a crime. There are things that must not be called into doubt, and among those are certain rules of life.

He had always taken other people's respect and consideration for granted, though there are naturally aspects of life that ought to be kept under wraps. He, Francisco Soler, was a man of good breeding who had been taught not to lift the lids off certain silver platters. Anything else would constitute a joke in poor taste, or the inappropriate behaviour of strange folk.

That German doctor, for example. He took keeping his mouth shut to such an extreme! He might at least pretend to make friendly conversation. The distance he put between them called to mind an isolation cell. Supermen, was that not what they had pretended to be? They deserved no better than to be treated with touristic curiosity.

In an attempt to calm down, Soler looked out at the winter sky, framed by the surrounding buildings. If he leant slightly in the chair he could make out the white paved paths of Plaza San Martín. That window in the grey building over there was the bedroom of uncle Octávio's apartment, where Soler usually ate lunch on Thursdays. In the building on the opposite corner lived the Donaldsons, excellent companions from the bridge club. He sighed, relieved.

That silent room irritated him. He had always used conversation as a protective screen. When one does not know what to think, one speaks. That is common sense. Or one makes love. Or, failing that, one drinks. Anything to stop oneself sinking into the bottomless and torturous pit of thought. The German doctor seemed to be at peace with his own conscience. Did he too give the impression of indifference? It had never occurred to him to confront others with a solid screen of individuality.

In that living room crammed with plush furniture and porcelain, the ghost of solitude pulled horrible faces and unfurled its many threatening tentacles. He got up to examine one of the pictures. Did Luchter think him so guilty that he did not deserve a word of solidarity?

The engraving showed a female nude, a figure with both hands outstretched, as if she were being handcuffed. Surely he was mad if a female body suggested such an idea!

And why not? He had always feared women. If one allowed them too much importance they become a prison, that was certain.

Of course what he had said to the caretaker had been stupid. The man had surely repeated it.

As he slowly became aware of the dark presence of his fears, Soler felt his muscles relaxing as if someone were loosening the pegs of over-tight strings. At the same time another peg turned in his stomach until it became a knot tugging on his brain.

Why had he got angry with Czerbó that day? It was silly and they would never believe him. He did not understand what he had meant to say, but he thought the Bulgarian was overstepping the mark, so he'd asserted his masculinity in throwing him out of his house. The "ladies" who visited him had nothing to lose. He had to humbly accept that. His affected ways were no more than theatrics. Could he say that to the Magistrate? Could he say that an epidemic of necrological exhibitionism had spread through the building, and that he was invariably the victim? He remembered the tall figure and abundant grey hair of Dr Corro, who he'd seen passing when he was walking towards the inner rooms. He looked like the lion in the advert for Ferro Quina Bisleri tonic he remembered from his childhood. How would a lion take the joke?

Dr Corro lowered his handsome head between his shoulders with the patient attitude of someone whose job it is to listen. On either side of the office, Lahore and Ericourt adopted airs of feigned indifference. Soler was smoking one cigarette after another and lining up the matches in the ashtray, failing to understand why his gestures seemed of such interest to the Superintendent and the Inspector. What was he doing wrong?

"And when I went in with señorita Czerbó, I knew her brother was dead as soon as I saw him. I called the police straight away. It was eleven thirty in the morning."

The precision of his statement was not insignificant. People with nothing to hide give a lot of details. Or do they?

Dr Corro's face expressed the same good-naturedness as a doctor encouraging a patient to share the detail he has omitted, which always proves to be the most important one.

Soler sucked hard on his cigarette, as if it were an oxygen tube rather than a harmless roll of tobacco. The question came at last.

"You had an argument with señor Czerbó some months ago. What was the reason for that?"

"I don't recall."

"Let me jog your memory. When señor Czerbó was in your apartment—"

Unforgivable! He should never have trusted the caretaker.

"I believe it was a domestic matter."

Soler was reliving his student days, when the examiner used to sprawl in his chair like Dr Corro was doing now and attack with fierce irony:

"Can't you tell us anything more, señor Soler?"

"Señor Czerbó's Spanish was so poor that I didn't clearly understand the reason for his visit."

"You understood enough to judge there was reason to get angry, to threaten him."

"I didn't threaten him! I told him to leave me in peace."

"What had he said to irritate you so much?"

"I believed he was alluding to my private life. It seemed to bother him that I received visitors at night. We all have a right to a private life, don't we?"

The question sought approval. "Sometimes we have the right but lack the time," was how Ericourt would have liked to respond.

"May I ask a question, sir?" said the Inspector instead to Dr Corro, who answered with a solemn nod. Ericourt turned to Soler.

"In the context of your private life, did you give anyone a key to the main door?"

"No, absolutely not. Never." Soler ran his gaze over the three men who were smiling sarcastically like an examination board considering whether to fail him.

Their three gazes converged on the ashtray. Dr Corro lifted his eyes. His head had sunk even further between his shoulders and he crossed his hands over his chest. It wasn't a restful posture. He was lying in wait.

"Why did you call the police rather than the doctor?"

Soler uselessly sought an excuse this time.

"I thought it would be better, what with everything that's gone on in the building."

"That will be all," declared Dr Corro.

Soler stood up and turned to go, mumbling a farewell. He felt like he was dragging something worse than distrust behind him. The tone of the interrogation suggested ridicule. He met Luchter in the hall.

"It's all a silly game," he said as if to encourage him.

Luchter paid him no notice. Soler carried on walking with his head down. He tripped on the telephone cable and gave it a kick.

"They've had me on," he grumbled, shooting a look towards the closed room where hours earlier he had come face to face with the mysterious and macabre sight of Czerbó's death.

*

"Señorita Czerbó called me last night to come and see her brother. I found señor Czerbó very agitated. He was suffering palpitations and obvious signs of nervous shock. I prescribed a tranquillizer for him. I took the prescription to the pharmacy myself. I was present when he took the prescribed dose."

Luchter spoke with the precise and regular beat of a hammer, shattering the expectations of the three men listening to him.

"How long did it take for the tranquillizer to have an effect?"

"Around twenty minutes."

"What did you do while you waited?"

"I believe I smoked a cigarette."

"Only one?"

"I think so."

"There was one in the ashtray."

"I smoke American cigarettes. Chesterfield. You'll be able to check."

"Did you see a piece of paper in the ashtray?"

"There was a piece of paper on the bedside table."

"We found it singed in the ashtray. It had apparently been burnt with a cigarette butt."

"Possibly. I didn't notice that detail."

"What did you do when Czerbó fell asleep?"

"I went home. But first I stopped in at señor Iñarra's apartment."

"Did you meet anyone when you left your patient's room?"

"No one. Señorita Czerbó had already gone to bed."

"Is it possible that señor Czerbó woke up later and took the poison?"

"Highly unlikely."

Lahore leant back in the chair, satisfied.

"And how do you explain the fact that potassium cyanide was found in one of the capsules?"

Luchter jumped in alarm.

"That can't be!"

"I assure you it is," said Lahore. "The ashtray and the glasses have also been analysed. The cyanide was only present in one of the capsules."

Luchter remained in thoughtful silence.

"It can't have been a mistake," he then said. "They're very careful at the pharmacy. I trust them absolutely."

"Did you know that señorita Iñarra had been visiting señor Czerbó at night?"

"Did she admit to that?"

"She did."

It is difficult to read disapproval on the face of someone so private, but Luchter's reserve transcended disapproval. He jangled something metallic in one of his pockets. He took out a lighter and lit a cigarette.

"May I?" asked Ericourt.

Luchter offered him a cigarette and then held out the lighter. His hand was firm.

"What do you know about the photographs?" he asked.

"What photographs?"

"Some photos of señora Eidinger were stolen this morning from the house in Villa Devoto."

Luchter frowned.

"How strange. I can't see how."

"We may well call you again, Doctor," announced Dr Corro. Luchter did not flinch.

"I understand perfectly. Should I wait at home?"

"For the time being, yes. That will be all."

Dr Luchter stood up squarely, almost to attention.

"At your service," he said.

He turned and walked towards the door, his shoulders now rounding under the weight of some worry. He stopped in the doorway.

"Has señorita Iñarra been arrested?" he asked.

The light falling broadly across his face showed the pinkish tone of his clean-shaven cheeks. He had evidently had a good night's sleep.

"She's in custody," Lahore clarified.

"At your service," said the doctor again before leaving.

"When I'm holding a ball of thread," said Lahore then, "I like to let it lead me out of the labyrinth instead of getting tangled in it like a damn kitten."

"That's what we're not doing," replied Ericourt. "If Luchter had burnt the paper there wouldn't have been a match in the ashtray. You saw he uses a lighter. The person who burnt the paper wanted to turn it into evidence against whoever wrote it."

"But how could anyone make a sleeping man ingest cyanide?"

"Have a look in the bathroom and see if you can find a dropper, the kind used for nasal drops."

Dr Corro shot him an amused look.

"I know it's not my idea. Plenty of people have read *Hamlet*."

Lahore shook his head.

"I'd prefer to question that young man, the one from the laundry."

"Come on, Lahore," concluded the Examining Magistrate as he stood up. "Let's have a look in the medicine cabinet. Are you coming with us?"

"No, I have to pay a visit to señor Iñarra," replied Ericourt bitterly. "It's time for me to turn into a sturdy dove of peace carrying an olive branch, or if you'd rather, a space traveller following the orbit of the moon. I've been trying to see him for days."

"You've been very kind, señor Ericourt," said señor Iñarra. He was sitting in front of the desk in his bedroom. The tartan blanket covering his legs twitched on the left-hand side and his arm knocked continually against his body and knees. His ascetic figure seemed surrounded by an aura of venerability, which emanated from the antique furniture, the wood and marble crucifix, and the photographs of his parents, wife and daughter on either side of the bed. On entering the room one had the feeling of being cocooned in homely intimacy. The solid columns of family history upheld good manners, reticent courtesy and the amiable presence of the old man who now occupied his place as head of the family.

He had listened in silence to the Inspector's explanations. Would it not be wise to notify the family lawyer? Did his wife know the news? No? All the better. It was his place to tell her.

"Will you keep Betty overnight?"

"It all depends on the investigation. It's the Examining Magistrate's decision now. Did you not suspect anything of the relationship between your daughter and señor Czerbó?"

"With a daughter as secretive as Betty I've learnt to leave suspicion aside, but I know that deep down she's an honest girl. I could never believe she was involved in criminal activity. Appearances accuse her, nothing more."

Exactly the right words. In señor Iñarra's orbit, the moon could never represent a crime. He would never admit that his wife or daughter were made of the same human material that at times is governed by the instinct for destruction.

"Do you have a typewriter?"

"We do."

"On señor Czerbó's bedside table we found a partially burnt typewritten note. It reads 'you tonight'. Your daughter admits to having written it. She also says she didn't go out last night."

"I believe that."

"I will have to question your wife."

A pause. Señor Iñarra's voice sounded tired, but even his lassitude was kept within strict confines.

"I understand. Would you mind if that conversation didn't take place here? It's time for my electric treatment. Please excuse me."

He rang the bell to call his wife. From inside the apartment came the sound of curtains being drawn. Darkness was falling. Before turning the lights on, señora de Iñarra went through the ritual of shielding the rooms from the curiosity of passers-by. Colonial traditions on the third floor of a modern apartment building.

Gabriela entered her husband's room quietly and with her eyes lowered. Her withdrawn attitude absolutely contrasted with Betty's arrogance.

"Did you want something, Agustín?"

"Señor Ericourt wants to speak to you. But first I'd like you to help me into bed so I can have my treatment."

"But you won't be able to manage it alone."

"I can manage perfectly. Just come back in twenty minutes to turn off the machine."

"I'm sorry to be a nuisance. I can wait." Ericourt was beginning to adopt the same good-natured selflessness with which señor Iñarra resolved his conflicts.

"Oh, it's no problem! It is just that we're on our own because it's the maid's day off. Gaby will be with you right away."

Ericourt left the bedroom. He sat in the living-cum-dining room to wait for Gabriela. He ran his gaze around the room. Tall-backed Georgian chairs around an oval table. The classic scene where generations of children have learnt the terrible imperative of proper behaviour. The image did not fit well with that of suspicion, like a blurred, double-exposed photograph.

Gabriela took over ten minutes to reappear. Her husband was surely telling her what had happened with Betty. When she came in she was very pale.

"I'm all yours, Inspector." She had sat down in one of the armchairs and gestured to the other in front of her, as if receiving a visit. Her propriety was of a different kind to that of her husband's. Less cloying, all told.

"Has señor Iñarra told you why the Examining Magistrate has taken your stepdaughter into custody?"

"Well, yes, the gist of it." Gaby moved her hands constantly as she spoke. "I don't believe she's got anything to do with this business either."

"But do you know if she went to see señor Czerbó last night?"

"Betty didn't go anywhere last night. She turned in early."

"And what can you tell us about her previous visits to señor Czerbó?"

Gabriela blushed.

"I didn't know about them. If I had done, I would have opposed them."

"Would your stepdaughter have listened to your advice?"

"Betty is haughty and independent," Gabriela sighed, "I've warned her on more than one occasion to be careful."

"What can you tell me about the Czerbós?"

"Very little. I had a neighbourly relationship with them, nothing more."

"Can anyone else confirm that your stepdaughter didn't go out last night?"

"I don't know. You can ask our maid when she gets back, but I don't think her statement—"

She didn't finish the sentence. The room had suddenly plunged into darkness.

"My God!" shouted Gabriela. "Agustín's had an accident. Agustín, Agustín! Are you OK? Can you hear me?"

"I'm absolutely fine, Gaby. This ruddy machine has done its thing again. You didn't think to turn off the other lights in the house."

"Have you any matches?" Gabriela asked Ericourt. She raised her voice in the dark so he could locate her. "I left my torch in the scullery. I'll go and put this right. I'll need to change the fuse."

"Gaby, come here," called Don Agustín.

The light from the match broke a patch of darkness.

"Thank you," said señora Iñarra. "I'll come back for you right away."

There followed a few moments of dark, anxious expectation before Gabriela reappeared at the doorway.

"Come with me," she said, illuminating the room with a small pocket torch. "You can wait with Agustín."

Señor Iñarra was sitting on the edge of the bed. The torch lit up the short-wave apparatus beside him. Ericourt took a seat in a chair next to the bed. The beam of light slid over the walls and disappeared.

"My wife will have it fixed in no time," said Don Agustín jovially. "It's my fault for having used an amateur electrician. My daughter is right when she accuses me of being over-protective."

These last words acted as a *fiat lux*. The bedroom, suddenly reclaimed by light, presented Ericourt with a new sense of surprise. Gaby came in, and avoiding her husband's eyes, she spoke directly to the Inspector. She seemed bad-tempered.

"We can continue our conversation now, señor Ericourt." She had gone over to the desk and busied herself arranging some documents. "You'll have to wait to finish your treatment, Agustín. We can't keep señor Ericourt at the mercy of our domestic inconveniences."

Ericourt was struck by the uncomfortable sensation of being a stranger there, like when one watches an animated conversation without being invited to take part.

"I'll just trouble you for one more favour, if I may. I'd like you to show me the service rooms."

"Of course. This way," said Gabriela unfalteringly. "Be so kind as to follow me."

Her footsteps were as agile and quick as reflex movements. Ericourt followed her along the hallway, struck by how adept and active she was.

The scullery door opened onto the same hall as Don Agustín's bedroom. The service rooms were the kitchen, scullery and a narrow hallway that led to the maid's bathroom and bedroom.

Ericourt peered through the kitchen's interior window and carefully examined the position of the cornices and parapets.

"That'll be all," he said, turning round. Gabriela was waiting behind him, staring at the floor. She shuddered when she heard his voice. She must have been thinking about something else.

"Can I go out this way?" he added, pointing at the service door. "I don't want to cause you any more trouble."

Gabriela did not move from the scullery until after the Inspector had left. The bell was calling her to her husband's bedroom but she walked straight past and shut herself in her own bedroom, slamming the door to shut out the high-pitched, intermittent tinkling of the bell.

At the main door Ericourt came across Andrés Torres, who was busy hurling extravagant looks at his colleagues on the opposite pavement. They were all at their posts as if in defiance of the respective managements for having forbidden them from talking until the police interrogations had come to an end. Seeing him dressed in his blue uniform with silver buttons, Inspector Ericourt breathed a sigh of relief.

"Are you burning any rubbish at the moment?"

"No, sir."

"I need to go down to the basement to look for something in the waste."

The rubbish was piled up in the unlit incinerator. Torres, deep in the oppressive silence of protest, took off his livery and put on his leather apron and gloves. His reserved gestures belied the extent of his displeasure.

"What would you like me to look for, sir?" he asked, brandishing the iron fork like a sceptre.

"A spare fuse that was thrown down the incinerator chute."

People's modes of expression are limitless. Torres's head sank between his shoulders, speaking volumes. The soft sound of material being sifted was heard.

"There's nothing like what you're looking for in here," he said after a short while, standing up straight. The Inspector's small failure was ample compensation for him.

"Allow me," ordered Ericourt, snatching the fork from his hands.

"But Inspector, you'll get filthy. Take this at least." Torres removed his apron and went to put it on the other man. Ericourt ignored him. Among the pile of papers and scraps of food a shiny blue rectangle had appeared. Pushing away the scraps that covered it he saw it was a notebook with an imitation leather cover, almost the size of an exercise book.

"Caramba, señor Inspector, if you'd told me you were looking for a notebook I could've found that too."

Ericourt brushed off the cover of the notebook with his handkerchief. He put it in his pocket as if wanting to shield it from the caretaker's curious gaze, which was boring into it.

"It's fine. Tell me one thing: señor Soler's apartment is directly above the Czerbós's, is that right?"

"Yes."

Torres's face lit up. His expression changed instantly from resentment to amiability.

"Let's go," said Ericourt peremptorily.

An officer was keeping watch at the main door. He wouldn't move from there now. Andrés Torres had been right after all.

7

Where is Emilio Villalba?

The laundry was a small rectangular space, a corridor almost entirely filled by white counters and cupboards on one side, and shelves with red oilcloth curtains over the washing machines on the other.

"Can I help?" a woman asked Blasi. Her dishevelled head emerged from among the white canvas bags she was emptying. Her face looked as if it had been sculpted by a child from a ball of red clay. Her hair had all the charm of a wire brush that someone had attempted to fix in a perm.

"I'm looking for a young man who works here, your delivery lad. What's his name?"

"Why do you want him? He's not here."

Blasi showed his ID card. The woman's face suddenly changed colour. Now it seemed as if it were moulded from the insides of a loaf of bread.

"Wait a minute, I'll go and get my husband," she said, disappearing between the blocks of white enamel and glass where water, soap and clothes were dancing an infernal sarabande.

Her husband appeared, a rough man in shirtsleeves showing dense reddish hair on his forearms and at the top of his chest. He spoke with a Polish accent.

"Good afternoon, sir, how can I help you?" he asked in a syrupy voice.

"I'm looking for your delivery lad. What's his name and where does he live?"

"Emilio Villalba. He hasn't come to work since yesterday afternoon."

"Is he ill?"

The man raised his hands, opened his mouth and arched his eyebrows in a gesture that perfectly illustrated both irony and doubt.

"How should I know?"

"Quite easily, by asking."

"He doesn't have a telephone."

"Does he often miss work?"

The woman let out a laugh. She had not aimed to be cordial and had absolutely fulfilled this intention.

"Ha, ha! Half the week, at least. He'll be back."

"Is he the one who delivers to number nine, Calle Santa Fe?"

"Yes, he's our only delivery lad."

"Where does he live?"

"Wait a moment," said the man. He took a battered, stained exercise book out of a drawer. The place's neatness had its limits. The pages of notes revealed their assistants never stayed long in the job.

"Here it is. He lives at number forty-nine, Calle Paraguay."

"Thank you. If Villalba does show up, tell him to report to the police station," said Blasi.

The building on Calle Paraguay was a tenement like so many in the poor areas of Palermo, close to the railway tracks. On its flaking, faded front there was a sign painted with irregular black letters on yellowing wood which read: "Lodgings."

The woman washing clothes in the sink in the yard said Emilio Villalba had not been back there the previous evening or that whole day.

"Do you know where he might be?" asked Blasi. "Does he have family in Buenos Aires?"

"That one? Who knows! They come and go. There's a good reason I charge upfront."

"What kind of lad is he?"

"Same as all the others." The woman pushed a strand of hair out of her eyes with her forearm. "Round here all they talk about is their 'dead cert' bets."

"What are the names of his roommates and where do they work? You can at least tell me that." The slap of damp fabric which had so far accompanied the conversation suddenly stopped.

"Come with me to the store on the corner and I'll show you them," the woman suggested. "They'll be playing dice about now. If they're not there ask the storekeeper, he knows them."

They had not arrived yet, of course. Blasi sat down to wait for them in front of a glass of *caña*. He glanced around the narrow store with its boarded floor. The tables were shiny from use. The bottles placed untidily on the shelves suggested carelessness of ordinary routine. The storekeeper studied Blasi's movements with dark, evasive little eyes and his head tilted to one side.

Blasi did not get his hopes up. Like so many young men of his age and social standing, Emilio Villalba must have had only acquaintances rather than friends, people with whom he worked, lived or slept. His human contact would be limited to receiving and handing over laundry tickets from or to his employers or getting tips about the weekend races from his roommates. The kind of person who brushes past others every day, their lives as different as sun and rain. Distanced from one another more through indifference and overwork than they might be in time and space. Orphans of spirit, unable to build meaningful relationships, concerned only about their right to sleep in a bed, to eat and drink and enjoy their Saturday 'loves'. Selfish and protective of their meagre pleasures because they are the only things that give them a sense of the marvellous adventure God has bestowed on every man: life itself.

The notebook with blue covers lay open on Santiago Ericourt's desk, picking up the beam of light cast by the lamp with its green shade. More than a diary, it was a long, written confession that seemed to follow a series of sudden impulses. The dotted lines signalled different entries. Ericourt was rereading the pages.

"I do not know how much longer I can bear this torture. All my life I have been a coward, afraid to take responsibility for my actions, seeking the protection of others to solve my problems. This is how I was educated and fear has led me to live a constant lie, but what about him?

"It is some time since I have felt any pity towards him. I feel repulsed by his ability to put on an act and drag others into playing along. I ask myself why we have such fear of violence. Violence is as healthy as the electric discharges in the atmosphere. It is much worse to go on living a fiction as we do, breathing the foul air of a swamp. How else could we call the supposed tolerance that unites us?

. . . .

107

"There was a time when the word 'morning' held the fresh taste of freedom for me. Now it means nothing. Nothing can free me from myself. I tried it and failed.

"There is no use deceiving myself. I am a cowardly woman and my supposed freedom is a new form of cowardice. Everything scares me, he knows that. He must know the truth. Why does he not say anything? His silence makes him more contemptible in my eyes.

．　．　．　．　．　．　．　．　．　．　．　．　．　．　．　．

"Since last night I feel my life does not belong to me, as if I were a puppet whose strings everyone pulls as they please. I think the sympathy that drew me to Rita was a way of justifying myself. It is strange. However, people cannot bear to see their shortcomings in others.

"He knew. What he has tried to do is monstrous. Why am I so surprised? How could I have expected more from someone capable of taking pretence to such a degree of perfection? I envy Betty her ability to see the world with open eyes. At least she knows how to face up to her life.

．　．　．　．　．　．　．　．　．　．　．　．　．　．　．　．

"My God! Now I know why you have punished me. I have sinned against love, against sincerity, I lied when you gave me the strength to be truthful, you gave me the sense to renounce deception and I took refuge in it like the weak do. Sins against the spirit do not ever deserve pardon in your eyes, Lord."

．　．　．　．　．　．　．　．　．　．　．　．　．　．　．　．

The telephone was ringing insistently. Ericourt lifted the receiver. It was Blasi. His attempts to find Emilio Villalba had so far proved fruitless.

"Who's that?"

"The lad from the laundry. He was in the Czerbós's apartment." Blasi paused. "I found out he installed something or other at the Iñarras's place."

"Oh, yes!"

Ericourt was drawing geometric figures on a piece of paper.

"Can you hear me, sir? I've arranged to meet his roommates."

"Fine. Leave that. I've got another job for you. Come back here."

He hung up. He took his private folder out of one of the desk drawers. Idly leafing through, he ran his gaze over the different headings written in capitals: AGUSTÍN IÑARRA, GABRIELA DE IÑARRA, BEATRIZ IÑARRA, RITA CZERBÓ, BORIS CZERBÓ (crossed out), ADOLFO LUCHTER, GUSTAVO EIDINGER, FRANCISCO SOLER.

He slowly wrote another name on a blank sheet. He made sure the letters matched the handwriting of the previous ones: EMILIO VILLALBA.

He picked up the telephone and dialled an internal line.

"Sergeant Portela? Did the Magistrate send señorita Iñarra home? Did someone go with her? Perfect."

With a satisfied sigh he leant back in his chair. While he waited for Blasi to arrive he passed the time writing a few lines on the sheet he had just added to the report.

The shadow slipped into the Czerbós's kitchen. Rita was in her bedroom at the end of the hall, and the footsteps, although stealthy, rang out in the silence of her fear. Her hands desperately grasped the covers.

"He's back," she murmured in a strained voice. The words stuck in her throat and seemed to tighten around her chest like an iron ring. "They're back... they'll always come back..."

From the dark, empty space came faces contorted by torture. Faces that had one day smiled at her in her home far away in Germany, but had then been disfigured by death before disappearing forever from the world of the living. Rita trembled under the blankets.

"They'll always come back, Boris... I'm scared... I can't make them go away."

The footsteps had stopped. Rita fixed her eyes on the double-locked door.

She heard the click of a kitchen window catch. Fear vibrated in the air around her, and with it, the sound of a body sliding carefully through the darkness. The fear then intensified, paralysing her.

"Boris... I love you so much... you've been the only one for me... Boris..."

With her senses alert, waiting for the cloud of agony that would confuse all those images with that of pleasure, Rita repeated the name that had given her life meaning.

"Boris..."

She heard the distant creak of a window.

Rita then felt the iron ring split into lacerating, destructive barbs, like hooks in a torture chamber that swelled in her throat and tore a scream from her. Rita burst into semiconscious, hysterical sobs that convulsed her body.

She got out of bed and opened the door. Her teary eyes fixed on the door to Boris's empty room. With her plaits hanging down her back and her face bathed in tears, she looked very like a little girl who goes to her brother's room at night to say sorry for having made him angry that afternoon.

Yet behind the door there was nothing but darkness and silence. Rita didn't dare turn on the light. Boris's face was not there. That face, full of satisfaction when he made her scream by pulling her hair or sticking a pin into an insect, had disappeared from that room and that home forever.

"Boris, where are you?"

Rita went into the deserted kitchen, where the mysterious presence that had woken her filled the air with traces of fear. She went out into the service hallway. The black space of the courtyard drew her like the abyss of a dream. Arms trailed down the walls like long snakes, calling her. They were the same arms that used to grasp and grip her when she went to bed with her heart in tatters, having guessed from Boris's silence that the following day another of her friends would know the horror of betrayal.

She climbed onto a kitchen stool that was pushed against the wall, under the window. She leant out. From the kitchen window on the fourth floor, a rope dangled in the air like the questions she would never dare ask herself. The rope hung as far as the Iñarras's apartment.

What was life, after all? The fear of suffering? The fear of nothingness? Where was that nothingness? In Boris's eyes, which no amount of betrayal could ever fill? In the eyes of her victims? In her own inability to form a soul?

The others surely knew already. The others were those dead people, and Boris's persecution had opened the door to their knowledge. They knew because they had made the leap in space and time. Boris pushed them when he led them into the torture chamber and tore out their secrets. But his dead had not made him more powerful in life or stronger in spirit.

Yes, that black pit had to have a bottom. It was not possible to swing endlessly like the rope hanging from the window. In the Iñarras's kitchen, the shadow moved dimly and silently.

Rita felt the rope's pendulum movement hammering in her temples. She pressed her head with both hands and closed her eyes. The image of the dark pit expanded, then a bright spot appeared in that limitless shadow.

The cold wind of the winter night bathed her cheeks.

"Where are you, Boris?"

Her body rocked for a moment on the parapet and fell with a dry snap like the violent slam of a door. The rope quivered in the air. In the immediate silence before the building awoke, a hand emerged from the window of Soler's apartment and untied the rope.

Ferruccio Blasi entered Ericourt's office. The morning light picked out the yellowish sheen the sleepless night had left on the faces of the Inspector and his assistant. Blasi was carrying a bundle of papers.

"The fingerprints in the criminal record coincide with the ones found on the electricity box," he said.

Ericourt looked at the young man sympathetically.

"You've done well, Blasi."

"I can't claim I have, sir."

He evaded his boss's gaze. A sticky dejection had taken hold of him. He was exhausted by the previous day's exertion, the process of tracking people down to reveal their hidden sides, the permanently heightened mistrust needed to examine every action minutely. One ended up feeling the itch of doubt even with one's superiors.

Why had Rita committed suicide? What memories, what remorse awoke in her soul when she guessed at the secretive goings on in the building? The previous night Ericourt had instructed Blasi to slip down a rope from Soler's apartment and climb into the Iñarras's kitchen window to unscrew the cover of the electricity box.

Everything had gone well at first. He was even excited by the adventure, which had a savour of romance even if its motives were dishearteningly run-of-the-mill. The people best placed to deal with life are those who do not remove its heroic wrapping.

However, Soler's cheery willingness to lend his assistance had made Blasi uneasy, like when one suddenly lifts one's eyes and is surprised to find that the mirror returns one's own shameful grimace. Is that, then, how others see us?

Soler and an officer checked the sailing knot that tied the rope to the window. The officer threw the rope according to Soler's precise instructions, but it was Blasi who had to go through with it.

"It'll easily hold." Soler had examined Blasi's face after saying these words and left the kitchen, returning with a bulbous glass containing two fingers of liquor.

"Have some cognac to pep you up. And when you launch yourself out, move your body in time with the swinging rope, like when a horse starts trotting, but not too much."

Blasi was already climbing onto the marble table to kneel on the windowsill. He shot a reproachful look at Soler that made him blush.

"That's what we used to do at the English school when we wanted to escape at night. The experience did me proud a few years ago," he added glibly, "when an inconvenient husband came home unexpectedly."

"In my case I'm more likely to be the inconvenient husband," replied Blasi, "since my job forces me to work at night."

He wanted to make it clear that he was still on the other team and that this momentary collaboration was not as significant as Soler seemed to think.

From then on it was all ghastly, the shadowy space trapping the cold, his foot feeling for some support, his hands burning from the roughness of the rope, his body hitting against the solid darkness of the walls. Reality is in fact far more frightening and bothersome than it is heroic. Even Hercules' labours must have been disagreeable at the time.

It had not been pleasant. Any clue provided by the rectangular electricity box might prove painful for some, and on top of that there had been that terrible thud, breaking the silence like an explosion. His job was done, all he had to do was sneak out, not knowing who had thrown themselves out of the window or why. He found out later at the station. The colleague who told him did not look so utterly exhausted as he did.

"Poor woman!" he now said sadly to Ericourt.

"Poor woman indeed. Not for her death, though, but for what she did in life. I have the German police report here. Boris's photography studio was a front. His true profession was as a chemist, and during the Nazi regime he had been an informer. His victims were countless. Rita supported him."

"But why did she kill herself?"

"Who knows? Her brother's death must have been unbearable for her. She had given him her soul completely and with that she gave herself over to death. She couldn't carry on alone."

"It's a shame the circumstances didn't give us time to prevent such a terrible, unnecessary thing happening."

"The circumstances shape the investigation in their own way. We have to learn that lesson humbly. Is everything in order?"

"Yes," said Blasi patting the documents he had brought with him.

The file remained on Ericourt's desk. On the pink Manila cover there was a name: Iñarra, Agustín Pedro.

Blasi and Betty were waiting, sitting across from one another in the Iñarras's living room. Lahore and Ericourt had gone in to talk to señor Iñarra. Betty was pretending to read a magazine and Blasi scrutinized her reticent expression. Her reserve, even though she had once said her fault was that she trusted too much, must have stemmed from the deepest part of her nature.

How much of the truth did Betty know and to what extent had she used it for her own ends the day of her half-confession? She must have thought him very naïve to rely on him backing her up with silence.

Later events implicated her more than she had previously imagined. Did she know that appearances pointed an accusatory finger in her father's direction? Was señor Iñarra a maniac who, like many others, faked illness in order to cover up secrets and devious plans? Was she his accomplice, perhaps? What about Gabriela? What role did she play in their home, that of victim or instigator?

The relationship between Betty and Czerbó now seemed different to how it had first appeared but Blasi did not know whether that was a good thing. Looking at the young woman's wide forehead and distinctive nose, he told himself that friendliness could not be so deceptive. Yet Betty had not been friendly when he first saw her in the lobby with her stepmother. She dominated the scene with an air of complacency that must have been put on. Why did she not look shocked that night? A dead body in a lift in the middle of the night is not, after all, a common sight. Betty, he clearly remembered, had been keen to not appear worried and to distance herself from the situation.

It was clear that she had wanted to get hold of the photographs. She had surely destroyed them. Why? Who did they incriminate? Who did she want to protect? Betty barricaded herself in silence, the weapon of the guilty.

From the hall came hushed voices. Betty pretended not to hear them but must have been straining to listen to what they were saying. Suddenly there came a sharp scream accompanied by hysterical sobs. Ericourt appeared at the living room door.

"Come with me, miss," he said. "Your mother needs you."

The two men entered Don Agustín's room. He was sitting in front of the writing desk next to the window. The shadow cast by the anxieties of the past days darkened his face. The morning light emphasized the marks that the years and his illness had left on his drooping eyelids and wrinkled cheeks.

"Come in," he said by way of a cordial greeting, sweeping away the unpleasant feeling that the presence of those two men in his house must have caused him. "I'm very pleased you allowed my daughter to come home last night. I was sure this business would end well for her."

"This business hasn't ended," said Lahore. "We're here to question you and your wife."

"What? Why? I demand that you explain what's going on!"

"Perhaps we should let your wife explain it."

"She doesn't have anything to say to you."

"How can you be so sure?"

Don Agustín reluctantly rang the bell to call Gabriela. His left arm lay across his chest, the other hand grasping his wrist to calm the convulsive trembling somewhat. There was a knock at the door.

"Come in," said Don Agustín.

Gabriela's brief glance interpreted the scene immediately.

"What's going on, Agustín? Don't you feel well?"

"Don't be alarmed, darling." Iñarra's voice was as cold in giving the advice as it was in defence. "These men want to ask us more questions, although I really don't see why."

"Indeed, madam, I wanted to ask you what you did with the fuse you changed last night."

Gabriela gave him one of her meek looks that put her unconditionally at the disposal of others.

"I threw it down the incinerator."

"Would this be it, by any chance?" Ericourt had taken the notebook out of his pocket. "I checked the incinerator after I left your apartment yesterday."

Gabriela let herself fall into an armchair, her lips white and a look of horror in her dull eyes.

"It wasn't me," she said.

"We know it wasn't you. We found señor Iñarra's fingerprints on the electricity box. He told us yesterday, however, that you were in charge of repairing things that often went wrong in the apartment."

"Fine," said Don Agustín. "It was me. Last night when you were here I had the diary on my bedside table. I had taken it. I was afraid you would find it and attribute the wrong meaning to it, so I decided to get rid of it by throwing it down the incinerator. When I was in the scullery I feared you might have noticed my movements, so I faked the blackout by tripping the fuse so as to go back to my room without being seen. I took the torch Gaby had left in the scullery. That's all."

"Don't worry, madam, we can't arrest you for privately confessing to being afraid of someone you call 'him'," said Ericourt, maliciously emphasizing the words.

"My wife and I have had some difficulties, sir. I was trying to protect the privacy of my home. In these unfortunate circumstances people allow themselves to talk about others as if they don't have any feelings or problems. Gaby has exaggerated our situation. I don't blame her. The sheltered life she leads has affected her nerves."

"Is it your husband you refer to in the notebook, madam?"

"Gabriela, you don't need to answer that," protested señor Iñarra.

"What was the truth you were so afraid someone would discover?" Ericourt was unrelenting. Gabriela sobbed gently with her face in her hands. Her sobs suddenly grew louder.

"I was afraid this would happen," said her husband. "A nervous breakdown. Let me call my daughter to take my wife away and keep her company. I'm willing to talk."

*

"Poor Gaby!" said Don Agustín pityingly. "She's a weak-willed creature, easily influenced. That's why I've tried to behave like a father as well as a husband to her. Gaby has been so caring with my daughter that she won my affection from the first moment.

"She's dedicated herself to me ever since I became ill. I know the task of constantly nursing must be hard at her age. I've made an effort to lighten her load so she doesn't get exhausted, because her lack of moral strength makes her vulnerable. Uncharitable people have taken advantage of her exhaustion and dragged her into situations which, although not essentially ill-intentioned, could have turned out to be compromising."

"Who are you referring to?"

"Boris Czerbó. My wife told me. He tried to extort money from her. That's the situation the diary mentions."

"Why?"

"Things from the past. Before she married me, Gaby was misfortunate enough to be the victim of an unscrupulous man. Czerbó must have known that and tried to get money out of her."

"If you knew about it, why worry?"

Iñarra smiled wearily.

"My dear man, have you ever known a woman who simply tells the whole truth? They're very secretive when it comes to personal matters. They keep certain things quiet even in moments of great intimacy."

Don Agustín's voice remained moderately impassive, in the face of which any explanation by Gabriela would surely have come undone.

"My wife lied when she said she didn't know why Betty was visiting Czerbó. She confided in her, and Betty, stubborn as she is, decided to take the matter into her own hands and convince Czerbó that it wasn't worth attacking us."

Blasi came in at that moment. For the first time Don Agustín seemed filled with lordly amicability.

"Czerbó has died in mysterious circumstances," said Lahore.

"Ask our maid. She'll tell you that my wife and daughter didn't leave the apartment last night."

Ericourt began speaking again.

"I'm going to ask you some questions and I want you to answer yes or no to each one. Take notes, Blasi. I'd like señora de Iñarra to be present. Go and get her. We'll wait until she's ready to join us again."

Blasi found Gabriela in her bedroom. Betty was with her. The room had no personal touches. Gabriela did not seem like the kind of woman who finds it easy to express herself, so for her to confess what was happening in writing, the circumstances must have really affected her.

"I'll be right there," she said when she heard Blasi's request. "Stay here, Betty."

"I'm going with you," said the young woman irritably. "Why not call the maid and the caretakers as well? They'd hate to miss the show."

"Betty," reproached Gabriela. "He's not to blame."

"On the contrary, madam, I must accept some blame. I once allowed her to deceive me."

Betty turned her gaze away and took her stepmother's arm.

That way, together, they entered Don Agustín's bedroom and sat on either side of the bed. Señor Iñarra eyed them paternally.

After briefly explaining his intentions to Gabriela, Ericourt began questioning señor Iñarra. He stood with his hands in his pockets and was apparently absorbed in following the short trajectory of his cigarette smoke to the ceiling.

"Did you know that your daughter was visiting Boris Czerbó?"

"Yes."

"Did you know that the reason for these visits was that Czerbó was attempting to blackmail your wife?"

"Yes."

"Did you know the reason for that blackmail?"

"Yes."

"Have you ever been into Boris Czerbó's apartment?"

"No."

"Was your daughter at Boris Czerbó's apartment the night before last?"

"No."

"Did Dr Luchter come here after seeing Czerbó?"

"Yes."

"Did he tell you how Czerbó was?"

"Yes."

"Did you know Frida Eidinger?"

"No."

"Had she ever been to your home?"

"No."

"Is there any reason why you might harbour resentment towards your wife?"

"No."

"Is there any reason why your wife might harbour resentment towards you?"

"No."

"Do you admit that you caused the blackout the other night in order to get rid of some confessions your wife had written and which you deemed compromising?"

"Yes."

"Did your wife know what you were doing when she went to the scullery to change a fuse?"

"Yes."

"Did she agree to go along with your plan?"

"Yes."

"Did you know Emilio Villalba?"

"Yes."

"Did you know he had disappeared?"

"No."

"What other plan of yours has señora de Iñarra gone along with?"

Don Agustín looked disconcerted; Betty, indignant; Gabriela, expectant. Outside the window, puffy white clouds passed rapidly towards the west. An unexpected ray of sun momentarily lit up señor Iñarra's knotty, clenched fist. His negative response was heard once more:

"None."

Ericourt turned to Gabriela.

"Do you confirm what your husband has said, madam?"

She nodded her head.

"I'm arresting you, señor Iñarra. Your answers lead me to suspect that you are responsible for Boris Czerbó's death."

Gabriela's eyes filled with tears. Betty tried to put her arm around her shoulders but she shook it off as if the contact bothered her, then tipped her head back.

"Wait. My husband has answered with the truth, but not all

his answers are correct. I'm not sure if he's lying or simply doesn't know..." She paused. "Frida Eidinger came to our apartment."

"Gabriela!" Don Agustín almost shouted.

"Frida Eidinger died here, señor Ericourt." Gabriela was speaking with her eyes closed. "It's better to confess it all."

"Gabriela, you're mad! I won't let you go on." Señor Iñarra seemed very agitated for the first time and spoke in a commanding tone.

"You'll have to let me, Agustín. I've had enough. You're not going to frighten me now like you've always done. Now you can't do away with me like you wanted to. It would be too obvious."

"By God, Gabriela! What are you saying? When have I wanted to do away with you?"

The tension of the scene had made Betty turn so red it seemed she might lose control of herself. Iñarra, ensconced in his chair, hunched his shoulders to bear the weight of all the hatred his wife was spitting at him in the midst of her incoherent declaration.

"You wanted to do away with me because you knew that sooner or later you'd lose me. I'd discovered the secret of your eagerness to make me absolutely dependent on you. You made me feel I was irredeemably tied to a past I'd forgotten long ago, because while I was still afraid I wouldn't have left your side, right?"

Iñarra shook his head.

"Poor Gabriela," he muttered sadly.

"Poor Gabriela!" she repeated almost simultaneously. "Poor me. I was stupid to think this home would give me back the status I lost as a result of an unfortunate passion. How much you've needed me, Agustín! Only now do I realize what this farce has meant to you.

123

"What would have come of your cold, loveless life if I hadn't been here at your side, supporting you and giving you the opportunity to think yourself important by saving a poor woman with your selflessness?"

Don Agustín's face revealed a deep concentration. He suddenly seemed to remember that the others were there and with visible effort shook off the entrancement caused by his wife's words.

Gabriela spoke to Ericourt, now extraordinarily sure of herself.

"Frida Eidinger died here, as I said. She had asked to see me that evening to talk about something that was of interest to both of us. I received her because I had no option. She went as far as to threaten me with scandal."

"Why?"

"These people suffer from psychosis of the past," thought Blasi, "you can smell it in here."

Gabriela was shaking her head.

"I'd like you to consider how it was for me to have to bow day and night to the hand held out to me. I needed to live with something real rather than empty words."

Of course, everyone tries to justify themselves when they must admit to something like that, but it is often much simpler than they think and their mitigating circumstances never amount to much.

"It didn't make me happier," she went on, without clarifying what she was referring to. "My soul was as sick as his." She pointed to her husband. "I've felt terribly guilty towards Betty and him, they depend on me. And what's more," she paused and bit her lips, "he's just the same as us. He couldn't help me."

Don Agustín sank his head pitifully between his shoulders.

"Who do you mean?" asked Ericourt.

"Dr Luchter."

"Gabriela, I forbid you to mix other people up in your lies." Iñarra jerked his head up as if he had been stung.

"Leave her, Dad," pleaded Betty gently, "there's no point now."

"But I won't allow it. Dr Luchter is a friend."

"Friend? When have you ever had a real friend, Agustín? You've always looked for people you could help so as to tie them more firmly to you. You did that with Luchter, you protected him, advised him, and he eventually noticed me because I was different, because I didn't believe your lies."

Ericourt did not seem to be as pressed for time as Lahore, who was fidgeting nervously. He listened with his eyes downcast, as blurry a figure in the midst of the family drama as those clouds racing across the window frame.

"Dr Luchter has been my lover." Gabriela spoke these words fiercely. "If it makes you happy, Agustín, I want you to know I've tormented myself with all the remorse a person can feel. Every night I went to bed wanting to wake up and find it had all been a bad dream. I wanted to feel clean and innocent again.

"Lord, I've been so stupid!"

An instinctive horror paralysed Lahore. Like an inexperienced surgeon who sees diseased flesh and would like to tear the forceps from the wound and cover it back up under the falsely intact appearance of skin and muscle.

Gabriela continued in her clear voice:

"I'd been Luchter's lover for two years when Frida Eidinger arrived in the country. They'd had a relationship in Germany many years ago and met again here.

"I had no idea Frida Eidinger existed until the night she came to our apartment unannounced. I opened the door myself because our maid had gone to bed early, as had my husband. Betty was out and when she got back she went up to Boris Czerbó's apartment to talk to him. Czerbó had found out about my relationship with Luchter, I don't know how, and was threatening to reveal our secret if I didn't give him money.

"When I saw I was lost, I turned to Betty, who agreed to help me with her own money in order to avoid upsetting her father. That night, after Agustín went to bed, I sat in the living room to wait for Betty. Agustín knew I stayed up late and always made me a glass of whisky and soda. One, no more, so I wouldn't overdo it. He's like that. He keeps the bottle locked in his room. He says he has to look after me because I'm incapable of controlling my desires."

"It's true, Gabriela, don't hold it against me."

The words sounded like a pitiful plea. Gabriela ignored him, smiling disdainfully.

"The bell rang and I went to open the door. I found myself face to face with a woman I didn't know, who threatened to make a scene if I didn't let her in.

"Agustín's room, as you can see, is the last bedroom. There was little chance he would hear our conversation from there. Agustín never gets out of bed without my help. I agreed to the woman's request.

"Frida Eidinger came into my home like a woman determined to carry out a plan. She sat opposite me and told me her name. I'll repeat that it was the first time I'd heard it.

"She didn't beat about the bush in telling me what she wanted. She belonged to that class of person who knows no bounds when it comes to ensuring they have the upper hand."

"Or who assumes those bounds don't exist," interrupted Blasi, pleased to see Betty's childlike face free from any pretence.

A look from Lahore was enough to make him doubt how wise it was to make personal comments, but Gabriela was by this point so wrapped up in her own narrative that nothing would have cut her off.

"She told me Luchter was the only man she'd loved and for that reason she was prepared to win him back. She had weapons at her disposal and wouldn't hesitate to use them. According to her, I was in a worse position because I was jeopardizing a position that gave me the means to survive."

"What did you say to this?" intervened Ericourt.

Iñarra and Betty listened to the difficult confession like two stern figures on a tomb, their eyes trained on the floor. Gabriela with her calm, pained voice seemed to grow before their eyes, filling the scene previously occupied by the skittish ghost of her temperament.

On hearing Ericourt's question she shrugged her shoulders.

"I don't know."

"How can you have forgotten, madam?" Lahore protested crossly. "The words you exchanged that night must have been of the greatest importance to you."

"I don't know. I was too stunned," repeated Gabriela. "My silence must have exasperated Frida. She took a comb and mirror out of her handbag and started freshening her make-up, ignoring me."

"What did you do then?"

"I got up and went to the door. I was afraid Agustín might have heard voices and would call me to ask what was going on. He must have been asleep because his bedroom light was off."

"Is that true?" Lahore asked Iñarra.

"Yes, the light was off." The coldness had returned to Iñarra's voice.

"When I went back to the living room, Frida was putting her things away in her bag. She told me to think about her offer, smiling intolerably. I replied in the only way that could irritate her, with silence. She must have felt out of sorts because she went very pale and, taking the glass of whisky on the side table, drank it in one gulp.

"All of a sudden, I saw her grow paler still. She raised both hands to loosen the silk scarf around her neck, breathing heavily as if she couldn't get enough air. After that she leant back in the armchair, shooting me a look, like a desperate call for help. Then she took another deep breath and fell back against the chair.

"I rushed to take her pulse. It was barely there. I went to the scullery to get some water. When I came back she'd stopped breathing. I tried to get her to take a sip, but her mouth was rigid and she couldn't swallow. Her pulse had stopped.

"At that moment, all I could think about was protecting myself and getting her out of my home. I took Frida by the arms and dragged her to the door. There was no one in the hall at that time. I called the lift, put her inside and got in with her. I pressed the button for the sixth floor. When we got there I went to walk back down the stairs.

"That was when I remembered Frida had come into the building at a time when the main door was locked. Did she have a key to Luchter's apartment too? I opened her bag and saw the key ring. I recognized the main door key and was about to take it off the key ring when I thought I heard someone in the lobby.

Without hesitating, I threw the key ring down into the lift shaft and ran downstairs.

"When I got back home, I noticed the glass on the side table. I thought I should wash it to get rid of any fingerprints. While I was rinsing it, I asked myself for the first time, trembling with fear, what had happened. Had Frida committed suicide? Had she had a heart attack? When she was with me she hadn't behaved like a person desperate enough to kill herself.

"I turned off the tap. The water dripping into the glass was intolerable. I dried it and when I was about to put it back in its place in the cupboard, the light glinting off the glass winked at me in a sinister way.

"I remember all this because when I found out about the poisoning later, something flashed in my mind like the sharp light on that glass."

Gabriela's voice cracked. With a gesture of defiance she raised her head and carried on trying to control her trembling voice and hands:

"Then, for the first time, I wondered if Frida Eidinger was really the one who should have been poisoned that night of the 23rd of August."

"I don't understand it, Ericourt," protested Lahore, pacing across the Inspector's office, "I swear I don't understand. We've finally got a solution to the puzzle and you don't accept it."

"A solution? Señora de Iñarra's confession doesn't rule out the possibility that Frida Eidinger killed herself."

"I can't believe that. Señora de Iñarra poisoned her out of jealousy and then eliminated Czerbó so he wouldn't turn her in to the police. You're so cynical! She told us about her relationship with Luchter in front of her husband without batting an eyelid. A woman like that is capable of anything. Even of accusing her husband as she did."

"It might have been Don Agustín. The blackout he treated me to shows he's a man able to plan coldly and logically."

"You've got quite a way of complicating things with your deductions!"

"I'll admit I'm not intuitive," Ericourt said modestly.

"In my opinion," Lahore went on, "what we've got here are two different crimes. Gabriela de Iñarra knew Frida Eidinger would visit her that night. She might even have invited her in the knowledge that her stepdaughter wouldn't be home until very late. She must've asked Frida to leave Luchter alone and when she refused she went ahead with her plan of the poisoned whisky. Everyone would think it was a suicide when the body was found in the lift. Luchter would keep his relationships with the two women quiet, and anyway, it would've been very difficult to prove señora de Iñarra's involvement. No one would've seen Frida enter her home and no one knew about the affair, apart from Czerbó."

"And then she poisoned Czerbó to throw us off the scent?"

"No, there's something in the Czerbó case that makes me think señora Iñarra didn't do it. She would've destroyed the note. Whoever is responsible wanted to drag someone else in."

"And so?" asked Ericourt. His half-closed eyes shone with irony.

"All the neighbours have said Czerbó mistreated his sister. Perhaps she hated him, that's why she killed him. Señora Eidinger's death made her think of poisoning. Typical of the mentally weak. Her suicide proves her guilt."

"And in these shifting sands of hypotheses, what role does the disappearance of Emilio Villalba play?"

"Coincidence."

"Mention atavism and we'll have the complete picture of a conclusion which explains none of the events."

Ericourt took the private investigation folder out of his desk drawer.

"I have made a list," he said, "of the names of those implicated in this case and their possible motives for the crime. I believe we should call them all here for a reconstruction of the scene of Frida Eidinger's death, which will take place tonight. I asked the Examining Magistrate for permission, and Dr Corro has granted it. These notes are my version of that column 'The Value of Hope' from the horse racing pages."

He began reading out loud. Not a bit of uncertainty altered the expression on his satisfied face:

AGUSTÍN IÑARRA:

Why might he have murdered Frida Eidinger?

By mistake. He may have wanted to eliminate his own wife out of jealousy.

Is that possible?

Yes and no. He is too helpless a man to do without his wife's company. Gabriela's confessions prove that he was not unaware of her relationship with Luchter. Love may lead to a crime of passion in a case like this because the means are of no consequence when it comes to stopping the other person finding happiness elsewhere. Is señor Iñarra so deeply in love?

Could he have killed Czerbó?

Anyone apart from Luchter who had entered Czerbó's apartment would have had to sneak in via the service entrance. The locks were not forced, so whoever did enter the apartment to kill him did not do so by either door. But what if he had got hold of a key?

Señor Iñarra's illness makes such a feat implausible.

GABRIELA DE IÑARRA:

Why might she be Frida Eidinger's murderer?

Jealousy. She might have planned the crime and invited her over.

Could she have killed Czerbó?

This is probable if she did not kill Frida Eidinger.

BEATRIZ IÑARRA:

Why might she have killed Frida Eidinger?

She was determined to ensure her father's life remain peaceful and Frida constituted the most serious threat to her home. She could have poisoned the whisky. This is unlikely since it was prepared after she left the house.

Could she have killed Czerbó?

Absolutely. She could have climbed up to the Czerbós's apartment or got hold of a key. She knew what Czerbó was capable of. The similarity between the two murders seems to suggest they were committed by the same person.

RITA CZERBÓ:

Could she have killed Frida Eidinger?

She did not have any apparent motive for eliminating her.

Could she have been the one who murdered her brother?

Yes. Boris had killed her spirit. The desire for vengeance and freedom might have blinded her. She could easily get into Boris's room. Her suicide indicates that she could not bear the guilt, which is implausible in a crime committed by a resentful person who kills to win their freedom.

ADOLFO LUCHTER:

Could he have killed Frida Eidinger?

He might have done it to free himself of her persecution or out of fear that she would reveal his relationship with señora de Iñarra. He has admitted that he gave the main door key to Frida Eidinger. His alibi for the night of the 23rd of August is perfect, however.

Could he have killed Boris Czerbó?

Absolutely. He could have made the crime look like a clumsy attempt to incriminate him. The poisoned capsule and the half-burnt paper would be other evidence he fabricated to make it seem as if someone had entered Boris Czerbó's room after he left.

GUSTAVO EIDINGER:

Why might he have killed his wife?

Jealously. The neighbours have testified that their married life was not a happy one. He has admitted it himself.

As in the case of Luchter, his alibi is perfect.

Could he have killed Boris Czerbó?

Yes, if he was the one who killed his wife. But he would have found it more difficult than the others to get into Czerbó's apartment.

FRANCISCO SOLER:

Could he be Frida Eidinger's murderer?

He has no motive. His alibi is good.

Could he be Boris Czerbó's murderer?

They'd had an argument. Of all the people in the building he is the one who could most easily get into the apartment directly below his own.

EMILIO VILLALBA:

Why was he in the Czerbós's apartment? Why has he disappeared?

Was his presence in the Czerbós's apartment a mysterious sign meant to intimidate Czerbó?

A long pause told Lahore the reading had ended.

"The questions can be summed up in one," he said. "Where is Emilio Villalba?"

"Emilio Villalba is a pawn. We can make it checkmate with another more important piece. The question is: who killed Frida Eidinger?"

8

Who Killed Frida Eidinger?

Soot had smeared its greasy fingers around the kitchen. The oil-skin tablecloth smelt damp. A short, plump woman with a face as round as a coin was laying the table. A weak-looking young man sat waiting in a wicker chair. Even his cigarette smoke seemed to hang listlessly in the air.

"What's up with you, Mum?" he asked in a voice that made its way lazily through the garments on the clothes horse. "Is this target practice?"

The woman planted herself in front of him with her hands on her hips.

"What makes you say that, *che*?"

"You threw the knife like you were trying to get it into my mouth."

His mother returned to her pans.

"You'd better read the newspaper you've got there. Then you won't go asking me what's up."

"Off you go again. My old man was right when he said women—"

"You mention your old man whenever it suits. You're a sly one! What would he have said about taking on a lad we don't need? And a fine one you picked. Trust you to get one who's on the run from the police."

"Are you crazy, Mum?" The young man rested his elbow on the table and turned his head. "What're you on about?"

"Read about the crime with the German woman. They're looking for someone exactly like the lad you took on yesterday."

"Pah! You almost gave me a fright there." The son unfolded the newspaper and looked for the crime section. "You're great at twisting things. If you don't want to spend the money just say, and that's that."

"I've a mind to give you a slap, you cheeky sod." The woman carried the pan to the table, holding the handle with the edge of her apron, and poured the contents into two enamelled bowls.

"Read it, go on."

For a while the sound of spoons on bowls and the crackling of wood on the fire reigned in the silent kitchen. The mother peeked over at what her son was reading. He finally raised his eyes.

"You know, Mum, you're right," he said, now on the ball.

The woman turned red with fright.

"What do we do now, Omar?"

"Tell him to get lost. Do you want to get caught up in it?"

"Be careful. What if he realizes and kills us?"

Omar let out a terrifying cackle.

"Don't be daft! And lead them right to him? Don't talk rubbish!"

"Take the gun with you."

"'Course! What do you take me for? Get in the bedroom and lock the door, I'll be right back."

He went out into the dark yard. His boots crunched menacingly against the hard dirt on which a web of frost was already settling.

He went into the shed. The yellow cone from the lantern lit up a pile of sacks in one corner. A man with matted black hair was sleeping, half hidden by them. He jumped when he felt Omar touch his shoulder. Then he stayed very still, hunched in his rags, flattened against the shed wall like a praying mantis on a branch.

Omar scratched his head as he spoke.

"Look, *che*, I can't keep you on. My old lady's asking questions. She won't part with a single peso."

The other man listened attentively, curled up in his hideout. The words fell on his back like the cold drizzle that had whipped him on the walk from the village to the farm.

"You've no idea what my old lady's like when it comes to money. If you don't leave she'll likely go to the police, and the Superintendent listens to her because my old man wrote off a debt for him and he doesn't want her claiming it."

The other man's resigned silence gave him the courage to continue along his smooth-talking path of lies.

"Best thing is if you go early tomorrow before she gets up. Look, at four the freight train to Zapala goes past. Hop on, and off you go. No one will see you at that time. Have you got money?"

He noticed the lad's eyes shining with interest. A brief parenthesis between fear and suspicion.

"No worries, boss."

"Good." Omar felt better. The lad was just a poor devil, after all. Some ideas the old lady had. "Here's a hundred pesos. Go on like I told you."

"Sure, boss. No problem."

He had taken the money with a swipe and curled back up in rags and silence.

Omar crossed the yard clutching the gun, attentive to the slightest sign of footsteps behind him. He heard nothing. All that pursued him was the night, the cold and his fear. The shadows of apprehension closed around him, and opened for Emilio Villalba a path along which he could continue endlessly, leaving no trace.

The large group of onlookers was growing around the main door. Heads turned in time with the coming and going of the people gathered in the building's lobby. When the car stopped next to the cordon on the pavement, necks craned to see who the newcomer was. It was the kind of crowd that forms outside weddings and funerals with the same festive air of curiosity about either happiness or death. Deserters from boredom and everyday mundanity.

Aurora Torres assumed a ceremonial air, unconsciously playing the role of band leader from childhood *romería* processions. Overcome with excitement, she was forgetting a detail that tormented her—the detail with which she, in turn, had been making nights hell for her husband: the presence of the murderer. Andrés Torres was shooting Soler appreciative looks like the kind seen among the public at races when the favourite steps onto the track.

This sort of public display was at odds with Lahore's modest tastes. He was a man of order and preferred the routine of tip-offs and criminals with whom one used the standard procedures. His forced participation put him in a bad mood. He ran his ill-tempered gaze over the four people who were waiting on the brown velvet sofa: Betty, Soler, Luchter, Eidinger. Betty would play the macabre role of Frida. Another of Ericourt's 'ideas', since he maintained that the girl had shown herself to be a good actress the day the photographs were stolen. The image of the young woman, dressed in señora Eidinger's fur coat and multicoloured silk scarf, was like a punch to his retina. Her hands nervously clutched the suede handbag.

"Good evening," said Ericourt cheerfully from behind.

"I see no reason to feel so pleased," thought Lahore, "I can't say it's a professional triumph. We started with one death and now we've got three deaths and a disappearance."

Ericourt pulled him into a corner.

"Royal flush," he said in his ear. "I heard from the laboratory this afternoon. I now know where the cyanide was. I had my suspicions. Where were you? I tried to find you to tell you."

"Working," replied Lahore. "I've been following the trail of Emilio Villalba. He's got a history of theft in a butcher's where he worked. Where did they find the cyanide?"

Ericourt whispered a few words to him. Lahore shrugged his shoulders and shot a vague look over to where Betty was sitting.

"That's no great help to us."

Magnesium flashes from the cameras announced the arrival of the Examining Magistrate, accompanied by his secretary and a clerk. Both men stepped forward to meet Dr Corro.

The scene in the lift went smoothly. Betty watched impassively as the two men talked and Luchter went to open the handbag to possibly get rid of the compromising key ring. Soler repeated the movement that made the bag fall from the doctor's hands.

There were no questions. None of the actors exchanged words or made any gesture besides those strictly necessary. When the cameras focused on them, Luchter lowered his eyes and Soler smiled. Betty discreetly lifted the collar of the fur coat to shield her face, holding it away as if the warmth of the fur disgusted her.

Once the scene had finished, the retinue went up in the service lift to the Iñarra family's apartment. There the reconstruction would take place without the presence of journalists or photographers. The press had been told it would be nothing more than a simple interrogation.

Señor Iñarra and his wife were under police watch. A tartan blanket covered Don Agustín's frail knees, and he was freshly shaved and groomed. Gabriela looked like a defeated woman. She was dressed simply and her black clothes gave a greenish tint to her dark skin and eyelids, which were swollen from crying and lack of sleep.

When the retinue entered the living room, all eyes fell on Gabriela's dark face. A grimace of distress thinned her red lips. She and Luchter made no move to reach out to one another. The world of sensations that had united them for more than two years had brusquely shattered.

She got up, as if awaiting orders, with the same humble attitude she'd had when she came to that home years earlier, when Don Agustín's first wife was still alive and she did not want to become what the world calls a loose woman.

On the side table, next to the armchair where Frida had sat, they had laid out a glass of whisky, the silver cigarette case, the spherical lighter and an ashtray. On Ericourt's orders, all those present sat around the table. Señor Iñarra's hands clutched the arms of the chair. Everyone else smoked cigarette after cigarette. Betty took her place in the chair next to the small smoking table.

"If you please, madam," Ericourt called Gabriela, indicating the armchair across from where Betty was sitting.

There was a brief silence before Ericourt began speaking.

"I must tell you that this is not a formal reconstruction as such, because we do not know the true cause of señora Eidinger's death. The scene we shall witness will, in essence, be a line of questioning. We are making use of the scenario to better grasp certain details, which may lead us to a fuller understanding of the events. Some of you are here because your first statements were not entirely truthful and, as a result, you may have become accomplices by accessory.

"Señora de Iñarra, according to your statement, which was subsequently confirmed by Dr Luchter, it was untrue that señora Eidinger did not visit the building. She used to come at night, using a key that Dr Luchter himself had given her, but she only had a key to the main door."

Ericourt turned to Eidinger.

"You have stated that you suspected your wife of having relations with persons unknown to you. Were you referring to Dr Luchter?"

"I was entirely unaware of that relationship," said Eidinger.

"Before I go on, I must tell you that no photographs were stolen from your house. Señor Czerbó promised señorita Iñarra that he would stop his blackmail if she got hold of those photographs for him. She went to see you with the sole intention of getting her hands on them, which she managed. Our presence in the house made her think of faking a robbery. She tore up the photographs and threw them down the toilet."

Gustavo Eidinger's eyebrows arched in an expression of deep surprise.

"My God! I had no idea," he said.

"So we are faced with an incident," Ericourt went on, "which only subsequent events have led us to consider a crime. Without

Boris Czerbó's death and the disappearance of Emilio Villalba, Frida Eidinger's death could well have been a suicide.

"Señora de Iñarra was the last person to see Frida Eidinger alive. She states that she had absolutely nothing to do with the death by poisoning. Señor Iñarra also denies having put cyanide in the glass of whisky he served his wife.

"This rare circumstance has given rise to others of a criminal nature. The Examining Magistrate must collect all the elements of the case. One of the most important is the scene that took place here on the night of the 23rd of August.

"Those of you who knew Frida Eidinger are in a position to accept or refute señora de Iñarra's statements. Your observations may help us arrive at a verdict of suicide or murder.

"In fact, if we accept that Frida felt jealous of señora de Iñarra, we can also accept that she might have thought the battle was lost and decided to implicate her in her mysterious death as a peculiar form of revenge.

"Moving on to the second hypothesis: señora de Iñarra is an unhappy woman. Her family security is compromised because someone is blackmailing her. She trusts her stepdaughter, who offers to deal with the blackmailer personally. A new threat appears unexpectedly in the form of Frida Eidinger.

"Señora de Iñarra could have been lying when she said that the 23rd of August was the first time she saw the victim. She may have deliberately arranged to meet her that night.

"Why run the risk of meeting her in her own home? It wasn't easy for señora de Iñarra to find pretexts for going out. Perhaps she tried but señor Iñarra's sudden crises spoilt her plans. Eventually, at the other woman's insistence, she had to receive her at home.

"The third hypothesis is that señor Iñarra, also seeking revenge, poisoned the whisky to kill his wife. According to señora de Iñarra's statement, señor Iñarra knew what was going on."

Ericourt paused. The faces of Betty and her father bore remarkably similar pained grimaces; Luchter and Eidinger were very pale, and drops of sweat shone around their hairlines. Soler was shifting in his seat, waiting for the moment, which was taking far too long to arrive, when his name would be pronounced to explain why he was there.

"We have tried as best we can to reconstruct the dialogue between señora Eidinger and señora de Iñarra. I beg of you, madam," he said, turning to Gabriela, "please limit yourself to reading what is written here."

He handed a sheet of paper to Gabriela and another to Betty.

"This is your role, miss. Begin the dialogue from when Frida Eidinger enters the apartment."

Betty's voice sounded false. Gabriela's flattened accents and tailed off at the end of phrases. One could hear the scratching of the clerk's pen and Dr Corro irritatedly clearing his throat.

"I'm Frida Eidinger…"

As Frida's cutting replies cornered Gabriela and forced her to make up her mind, the two men who had loved the dead woman half-closed their eyes in gestures of tacit approval. The dialogue faithfully expressed Frida's true character.

Gabriela suddenly got up from her seat.

"Wait," she said. "I think my husband has woken up."

She went to the hall door.

"I stopped here," she clarified.

"Are you sure?" asked Ericourt.

Gabriela blushed.

"No, you're right. I went to the bathroom."

"To get the cyanide?"

"No, not that. I wanted to make sure Agustín was sleeping."

"Fine, let's carry on. What did you do then? What was señora Eidinger doing when you came back?"

"She was combing her hair. Then she reapplied her lipstick."

"Did she say anything more?"

"Yes, she told me to think about what she'd said because she wasn't prepared to back down."

"Was that when she drank the glass of whisky?"

"Exactly. She was already getting up to leave. She suddenly grabbed the glass and drank it in one gulp. I realized she was pretending to be calmer than she actually felt."

"Good, let's reproduce the scene. Be precise in your movements. You, miss," he added, addressing Betty, "will act as a woman readying to reapply her make-up. In the handbag you will find everything you need, nothing has been touched."

He was aware that the attention everyone was paying him oscillated between irritation and mockery.

Betty, who had opened the dead woman's handbag, took out the comb and smoothed her hair, then lifted the lipstick towards her mouth.

The standard lamp crashed to the floor. Someone had stood up brusquely and knocked it over. The incident was enough to make Betty pause with the lipstick hovering in front of her mouth.

"Don't be alarmed." It took Lahore a few seconds to realize it was Ericourt speaking. "Nothing will happen this time. We changed the lipstick in the laboratory. This one is not poisoned like the other one. You have given yourself up, señor Eidinger."

Eidinger scanned the room as if looking for a way to escape. Moving just as quickly, two police officers immobilized him.

"The facts themselves complete the investigation."

In a voice that was absolutely flat, as if his words had travelled a long way and emerged blurry with fatigue, Ericourt explained to Blasi the series of circumstances that led him to discover the author of the crime.

"I didn't like Eidinger the first time we went to visit him. He fiercely guarded his modesty, which to me seemed like patched-up hypocrisy. But what could I accuse him of? Earlier events puzzled me and inclined my suspicions towards the Iñarra–Luchter pairing. I later regretted that. Luchter is a true fighter, a man who strives to raise himself through his own efforts, not trampling others or their feelings in the process. As for Soler," he added disdainfully, "he's a blank canvas. Remove the frame and there's nothing left. Who could take him seriously?"

Blasi was listening carefully. Ericourt once more inspired confidence as a boss. He felt the relief of a child who is wholeheartedly convinced that his father's self-possession is not a capricious desire to wield power, but in fact the product of deep-rooted convictions by which one may live.

"When I learnt about the existence of the poisoned lipstick," Ericourt went on, "the circumstances led me to suspect Luchter. He might have disposed of the lipstick case along with the keys, counting on Soler not noticing and therefore not saying anything. Of course this was a risk, because it might have drawn attention to two elements that would have otherwise gone unnoticed. But there is always the possibility of a wrong move, and Luchter could well have made one.

"The fortuitous find of the poisoned lipstick ensured that reconstructing the scene of Frida's death would lead us to the criminal. It was logical to suppose that whoever it was would be afraid to see Betty wielding the deadly lipstick and would be faced with a terrible dilemma: if Betty used it, her death would betray the way in which the first crime was committed; if either she or anyone present stopped the gesture, the act would be equivalent to a confession. Eidinger was in control of his nerves up until the last moment, but the very concentration of his energies provoked the reflex action that was his downfall. They won't let me live this down," he added, stretching his lips now in a rictus that on someone else would have been a smile. "Sensationalist is the gentlest adjective that has been applied to me. I must admit that I like a bit of sensation. My aesthetic instruction dates from the first decade of the century.

"The case of Frida Eidinger," he went on almost without pause, "is one of a passionate obsession and its resulting resentment and devastation. Frida married Gustavo Eidinger for the sole purpose of leaving Europe and coming to Argentina, where Luchter had been living for some time. She was obsessed with the idea that only with him could she find happiness.

"But Gustavo Eidinger's plans also depended on her. He needed his wife's money to live the kind of life he considered essential. Divorce would be a disaster for him. Don't forget that the marriage took place in Switzerland, at Frida's request, and as such the dissolution of the marriage in any country allowing divorce would strip her husband of any right to a potential inheritance.

"Gustavo Eidinger acted like a spoilt child. He uses others but cannot bear the thought of being used himself. In the case of his marriage he could only tolerate failure while taking advantage of the external situation to convince himself that 'everything had turned out well'. Can you imagine the effect Frida's confessions must've had on him? His perfect plan was failing and he learned that someone else was, like him, capable of coldly using others. His spite swelled until it led him to plan his wife's death.

"The two adversaries in this conflict were very similar. Husband and wife shared the same cynicism and unscrupulousness. Frida Eidinger was one of those women who spend their lives dealing out moral blows under the pretext of being frank, as an outlet for their aggressive instincts.

"What could she have done to more brutally hurt her husband? She simply announced her plan: she told him she would divorce him to marry Luchter. As if in a game of skittles, she wanted to knock down the last pin of Gustavo's personal defences. Frida was a woman capable of twisting a chicken's neck in front of a sensitive child and then saying it was to strengthen his character. We have somewhat forgotten the meaning of old words, but ferocity will continue to be the most appropriate.

"Eidinger knew Czerbó. His own wife must've told him about the advances he'd made as a chemist in Germany. The police report showed that Boris was an instructor for the student group of which Frida was a member. This explains his subsequent interest in getting hold of the photos.

"Eidinger got in touch with Czerbó. He needed a way to eliminate Frida without creating suspicions. Czerbó had managed to fix potassium cyanide in a solution that could be incorporated into the carmine used to make lipsticks and other materials. Eidinger suggested making a poisoned lipstick, which he then substituted for his wife's. He had promised to pay a hefty sum when he inherited Frida's estate.

"But the circumstances of the death complicated things. (Frida carried that lipstick in her handbag because she had another one on her dressing table.) Anywhere else, señora Eidinger's death wouldn't have caused any bother for her husband or for Czerbó. It would've been seen as a suicide and it wouldn't have been difficult to get rid of the compromising lipstick. In Luchter's apartment, it would've only caused problems for him.

"The appearance of the body in the lift, Luchter's perfect alibi, and the mysterious visit to señora Iñarra meant further dangers for Eidinger. He had to get rid of Czerbó and make us suspect it was a double crime for reasons of political revenge. Meanwhile, Czerbó wanted to get hold of the photographs because if reports were requested from the German police about the organization, it would become clear he had a previous connection to señora Eidinger and his situation would thereby become very dangerous.

"To eliminate Czerbó, Eidinger needed to get into his apartment and hide until both brother and sister went to bed. He knew their habits. The Czerbó siblings used the service quarters as storage space. Hiding there for a few hours wouldn't be impossible. He planned to dissolve the cyanide in a glass of water and swap it for the one on Boris's bedside table so he would drink it when he woke up. If his plan worked, no one would suspect him because it was difficult to get into the house. People would probably assume it was another suicide.

"All he had to do was get hold of a key for the apartment's service entrance. Eidinger could move about freely, no one was watching him. It only took him a morning to find out which suppliers regularly ran errands in the building.

"That same day he found out personal details about them and chose Emilio Villalba, an unintelligent young man without any family, who needed money because he was fond of the races. He bribed him to get a wax impression of the key for the service door on the third floor. Emilio Villalba did this while Rita was looking for the supposed lost ticket.

"Eidinger didn't waste a minute. He waited for Emilio Villalba in his car and drove him, after he'd handed over the wax impression, to a bus station, giving him enough money to pay for his bus fare and his silence. A poor devil doesn't go to the police when he'd do better to hide from them.

"He returned home. In his workshop he had a casting kit he'd bought from a hardware shop in another neighbourhood away from where he was going to carry out the last and most dangerous part of his plan. He made a copy of the key, and conveniently disguised, but not so much as to arouse suspicion (a pair of glasses, a moustache, a roomy overcoat to alter his figure), he entered the building on Calle Santa Fe when people's movements were not yet being monitored by Torres's peasant-like suspicions, and hid in the Czerbós's service room.

"From his hiding place he heard Dr Luchter talking to Rita in the kitchen. Luchter said he would go to the pharmacy to have some capsules prepared, which he would personally give to Boris, and told her she should go and rest.

"Luck was on Eidinger's side. After taking the calming dose the patient would fall deeply asleep, the doctor said. Eidinger decided to change his plan and not wait for Boris to drink the water in the morning. It occurred to him to look for a dropper in the bathroom and administer the poison through his nose.

"When Rita gave her statement, all indications would point to Luchter. Eidinger silently carried out his plan, and Rita, behind the locked door of her room at the other end of the hall, could not hear him. Then he returned to the scullery, carefully washed the glass in which he had dissolved the poison and put everything back in its place. Finally, to further implicate Luchter, he opened one of the capsules and substituted its contents. He naturally took the precaution of wearing rubber gloves.

"The following day he called the police to tell us about the mysterious threat he had received, so as to make Frida's death seem like a crime between ex-associates. Luchter and Czerbó, being German and former residents of Germany, would be implicated. Not even the discovery of the poisoned lipstick could incriminate him then. The presence of Betty and the fake theft of the photographs helped him further. Eidinger was sailing with the wind in his favour."

"If Czerbó had decided to act earlier, or if Betty had talked," said Blasi, "Czerbó wouldn't have died, nor would Rita."

"There's no need for such regrets. The Frida Eidinger case would probably have been classified as a suicide. Time crystallizes facts but the measure of that time does not belong to man."

Blasi seemed unwilling to get involved with his boss's philosophical musings.

"How has Betty taken it?"

"Well, the charges against her are minor. Her home will soon get back to normal. Don Agustín is busy saving Gabriela and

150

in the meantime suffers new crises. She, meanwhile, becomes the angel of the house."

"But is Don Agustín very ill?"

"Ill enough to convince himself he cannot be left alone."

"Poor Betty! What a way to come unstuck! A scandal was the last thing she wanted."

"Those are grand words to hide the excessive desire to meddle she inherited from her father. There's nothing wrong with sparing the suffering of those we love, but someone should tell your pretty protégée that she'd do well to be modest and not claim such a role in the joys or misfortunes of others."

"That's a good idea," Ferruccio admitted. "I'll call her as soon as I'm free."

"To tell her?"

"No. To ask her if she'd like to go for a walk. We owe it to Muck."

———

AVAILABLE AND COMING SOON
FROM PUSHKIN VERTIGO

ALSO AVAILABLE FROM PUSHKIN VERTIGO

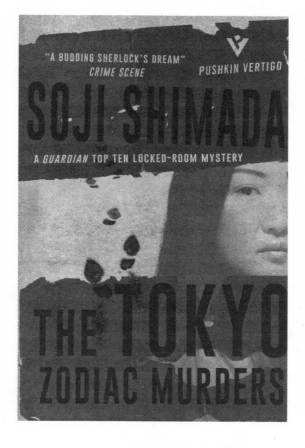

Find out more at **www.pushkinpress.com**

FRÉDÉRIC DARD

PUSHKIN VERTIGO

DEADLY DECEIT IN '60s
PARIS, FROM THE
UNDISPUTED MASTER
OF FRENCH NOIR

BIRD IN A CAGE

Find out more at **www.pushkinpress.com**

'THE FRENCH MASTER OF NOIR' *OBSERVER*

PUSHKIN VERTIGO

FRÉDÉRIC DARD

THE WICKED GO TO HELL

A PARANOID PRISON-ESCAPE THRILLER FROM
ONE OF FRANCE'S MOST POPULAR WRITERS

Find out more at **www.pushkinpress.com**

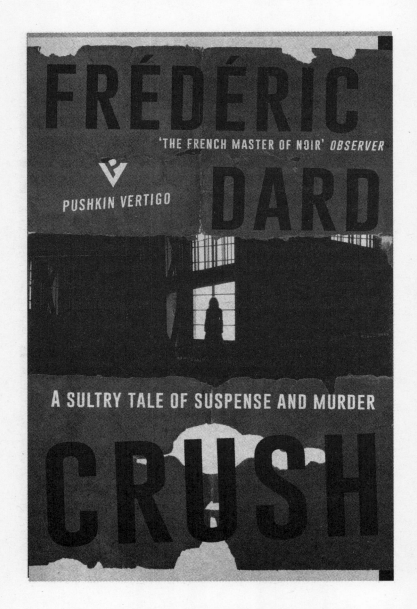

FRÉDÉRIC

'THE FRENCH MASTER OF NOIR' OBSERVER

PUSHKIN VERTIGO

DARD

A SULTRY TALE OF SUSPENSE AND MURDER

CRUSH

Find out more at **www.pushkinpress.com**

'ECHOES OF CHANDLER...A REMARKABLE
DEBUT' *BORÅS TIDNING*

Find out more at **www.pushkinpress.com**

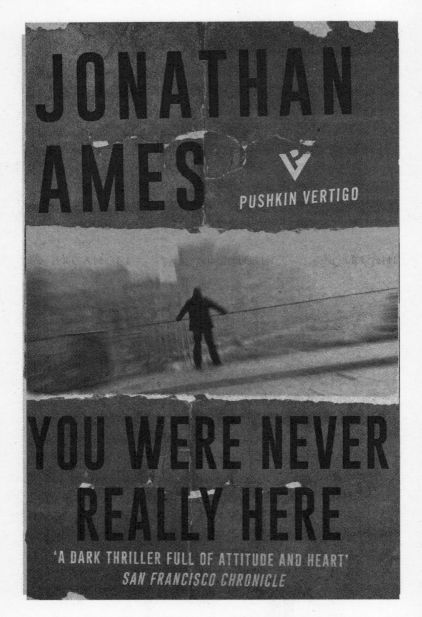

JONATHAN AMES

PUSHKIN VERTIGO

YOU WERE NEVER REALLY HERE

'A DARK THRILLER FULL OF ATTITUDE AND HEART'
SAN FRANCISCO CHRONICLE

Find out more at **www.pushkinpress.com**